GAMES
OF PASSION

I would like to dedicate this book to my grandmother, Louvenia Webber that recently celebrated her 100th birthday; family and friends that helped, inspired, and supported me during this entire project.

This book is also in memory of my grandmother, Avolia Howard, who passed away back in 2008. She will forever be in my spirit and serve as a key storyteller in my life.

Acknowledgements

I would like to thank all the contributors to this book for their time and expertise. I am grateful for your creative energy for this project from the beginning to its completion.

Finally and foremost, I want to thank my cousin and lifetime friend, Danny Howard, who has seen me through my rollercoaster ride of successes and failures.

THE LACE
COLLECTION

GAMES
OF PASSION

FRANK LEE
SPEAKING

Pages

My words, my thoughts, their meanings tell my story; random choices for a carefully conceived but unraveling episode. Pictures show faces, music take me places while my thoughts possess my mind. Blank sheets fill the blank pages of the book of my story. I do desire to command the pen that orchestrates the words that form the meanings. My words may be clever but my message is simple. Search the drawers that hold the secrets. If they are drawers, why are they holding the contents of my possessions instead of drawing artistic sketches, expressions, or conclusions like those that the name implies? I'm confused at this point.

Now, I will return to the blank pages that lead to an empty middle and uncertain ending. Wait! Turn the pages. Change the story. The pen is my magical wand.

Frank Lee Speaking

CHAPTER 1

"MR. Howard, the flight will be taking off shortly. We have a delay with the tower," the captain said.

"Let's get this show on the road. Chop! Chop! Time is money. I need to be in New York in 4 hours," Lance replied as he tapped his hand on the mahogany table, checking his watch, and looking out the window. Seconds later, he checked his watch again as if checking would make time go faster.

[Ten minutes later]

"Mr. Howard we have clearance to takeoff. We will be airborne shortly."

"It's about damn time."

The flight departed LAX at precisely 6:03pm.

The plane finally reached cruising altitude of 38,000 feet. Lance looked out the window into the abyss of darkness; sorting through his barrage of thoughts from the previous day.

"Would you like a drink Mr. Howard," asked the flight attendant as she lightly touched him on the shoulder to get his attention.

"Yes, bring me a dirty martini", turning his head to glance up long enough to make eye contact before looking back out the window. He turned his head again in her direction again as he noticed her short, tight skirt, skin colored panty hoses, and flat loafers as she walked toward the bar.

Shortly, she returned with his dirty martini and napkin, placing them delicately on the mahogany table.

"What's your name," he asked as his eyes narrowly followed her womanly curves from her loafers, over her skirt, gazing at her generously exposed breasts as she leaned carefully placing his cocktail on the table.

"Candice," she responded with a half-smile.

"What a sexy name; it's one of my favorite. It just rolls off my tongue so smoothly", as he licked his lips from his half opened mouth.

"Thank you", her eyelashes blinking more than normal; eyes turned upward, and her mouth parted to show her teeth.

"Thank you, Mr. Howard."

"Call me Lance", sitting back into his chair, leaning his head on the rest while swirling the frigid liquor in his glass.

"How long have you been a flight attendant?"

"About seven years. I started flying right out of college."

"That's a long flight", as he made eye contact watching her eyes roll; shaking her head and smiling.

"I see you have a sense of humor. Do you always make people laugh?"

"Not always. Sometimes, I make people cry but not every day."

Her eyebrow arched upward and eyes widened. She wasn't sure if he was being serious or continuing his banter. She wanted to learn more about this playful but focused man. Since it was a four-hour flight and she wouldn't serve him dinner for another couple of hours, she seized the opportunity to learn more.

"I'm afraid to even ask what that statement really means. Anyway, what kind of work do you do?"

"I do 'computer stuff.'"

"'Computer stuff!' What kind of 'computer stuff,' she asked with a smirk.

"I'm an application developer for sharing videos. Are you computer savvy?"

"Not really. I play around online, but for the most part, I just know the basics."

"Basics are good. What do you do for fun?"

"I like to go dancing when I have down time. I relax by going to the beach. I'm from San Diego, so that makes it easy", as she smiled giddily.

"What about you?"

"You said who or what do I do for fun?"

Candice eyes rolled while blushing as she shook her head. "I said what do you do? I see you have jokes."

"I swim, water ski, sky dive and read."

"That is an odd combination of things, but if it works for you, it works for me."

"So what's the wildest thing you have seen since working as a flight attendant?"

"Not a lot of unusual things. I saw one passenger get drunk on a commercial flight and wanted to undress in public. On a private flight, I saw strippers dancing and 'entertaining' the plane's owner."

"Have you seen any instances involving the 'mile high' club," as he casually sipped on his martini.

"No, but I have heard anecdotes from my colleagues. Would you like another martini?"

"Yes, please!"

Candice moved with celerity toward the bar, as if she had something urgent to do. She exhaled and paused for a moment, while her imagination took her down an erotic trail. She always wanted to join the 'mile high' club but never dared. I can't believe I'm even entertaining these thoughts. I'm a flight attendant for God's sake. I would lose my job, a job that I love. Besides, I don't even know him, as she took another deep breath before returning with his drink.

"Mr. Howard, here is your drink."

"Oh, I'm Mr. Howard now. Where is that warm and convivial flight attendant that was just here having a conversation with me. Management!" as he raised his hand to gesture to an imaginary authority figure.

Candice blushed and burst into laughter as her eyes rolled and hand rubbed along the nape of her neck.

"You are too much."

"No, I'm just the right amount; unless you say when."

"To what?"

"When to stop", as he gazed into her eyes, he rose from his seat and walked pass her, heading to the restroom.

She was speechless as the whiff of his intoxicating cologne and masculine scent tempted her remaining self-control.

Candice sharply turned her head to get a good look at Lance's brawny athletic body. At 6'2," Lance's statue owned the confined space with a presence exuding an animalistic, virile nature. While Lance was away, Candice seized the opportunity to get out of this enticing but precarious situation.

Lance was exiting the restroom as Candice continued washing the glasses and stowing away the other containers. As she kneeled down to stow the shakers, Lance got a revealing view as he noticed a tattoo on her thigh.

"I see someone has an undercover exotic and adventurous spirit."

"What do you mean?"

"I noticed your tattoo; what is it", as he leaned against the counter.

"It's a paw print."

"Interesting; am I the prey or are you the predator?" as he rubbed his chin.

"OK," as she turned around to continue cleaning the remaining containers from the martinis earlier. Lance walked closer until he could see the fine hair along the back of her neck.

"Where do those paw prints lead: Am I the prey or are you the predator?" he whispered in a deep huskily voice.

Candice's whole body quivered as a tingling sensation ran up and down her spine. Her sinful thoughts exploded.

She could feel Lance's breath on your neck. He was close. She could smell his cologne. Why was this man that she barely knew, invading her personal space and whispering things in her ear, and taking up way too much "real estate" in her head?

Candice worked a lot. Her hectic lifestyle didn't allow much time for a traditional relationship. She dated a few local guys but nothing serious. The guys that she dated were more convenient sex partners than anything else. Working the private chartered planeside of the business left her little time for a normal schedule. At a moment's notice, she could be flying from one side of the country or the world to the other without any notice. Although she was handsomely compensated, and enjoyed the traveling lifestyle, sometimes she wanted to come home to a man or spend quiet weekends with that special someone relaxing. Right now, she was in the midst of a precarious situation, and she enjoyed the attention.

As Candice shivered and turned around to face Lance, surprisingly, he pulled her close and gave her a kiss, tasting her luscious lips. He pressed his rigid, muscular body against her voluptuous, 38D breasts. His strong hands traced the curves of her womanly features.

"I can stop if you want me to," he whispered in her ear as the tip of his tongue teased her ear lobe. Candice's eyes were still closed and her breathing shortened as the two of them separated. She put her fingers over Lance's mouth. She exhaled as she turned to face the sink, attempting to regain her composure. Lance rubbed over her curvaceous hips as he pressed the issue.

"You didn't answer my question."

Moments later, she turned around and licked his face as she grabbed his ass. She continued kissing him passionately teasing his mouth with her tongue flickering it quickly in and out of his mouth. She whispered in his ear—"Does this answer your question?"

Lance pressed Candice against the counter as his hands raised her tight skirt to expose her turquoise colored lace thong panties. He grabbed her ass as he grinded his hips against her soft wetness. His hands traced the inside of her thighs as he lifted and placed her on the counter. She grabbed his head and pressed his face into her buxom breasts. Lance grabbed a handful of breast and licked the tip vigorously as he fixated his eyes on Candice's face; watching her every reaction. She panted as his tongue teased and ignited a sizzling sensation.

"Uh, uh!"

"Yes, lick it!"

"Suck it!"

"Don't stop!"

"Don't stop!"

"Lick the other one!"

"Oh yes!"

"Suck on it!"

"Bite it!"

Lance flipped her over, slid her moist thong aside, and thrusted deep inside before pulling his cock out. Candace moaned; gasping for air and rolling her eyes, as she leaned her head back.

"It's not wet enough. I will slide it back inside when I think it's wet enough."

"Baby no! Don't make me beg! I need it!" Candice was both hungry and thirsty for Lance at this point. Lance made her beg anyway. He loved to make women plead for pleasure. Making women plead was his way of "stroking" his ego. Candice would not be the exception. He planted the "seed" in her imagination and watched it flourish.

Lance mentally returned to pleasing Candice. She was begging as her body craved him. Lance dropped to his knees, nudged her thighs aside, and explored her plump pussy lips with his tongue. He worked his way up to her clit. After sucking on it for only a minute or two, she began to cream.

"I think it's wet enough now. Can you feel me inside." as he slid his hardness back inside of her. Lance bent her over the counter as he grabbed her shoulders pumping her harder and deeper with each thrust. He raised her skirt exposing her round ass. She had a symbol tattoo at the base of her back. Lance grabbed, squeezed, and slapped her ass as he furiously penetrated her. Candice chest rose and fell as Lance drove inside her hard and fast. He took his fingers off her shoulders and grabbed a handful of her ebony colored hair as he pressed her down on the counter. Her hands pushed against the wall with each of Lance's manly thrusts. Candice arched her back and moaned loudly sounds of ecstasy. Lance licked the back of her neck and sucked on her earlobes as Candice turned around to give him intense kisses as he pumped her.

Moments later, Candice slid her soaked panties off, un-snapped her bra, and got on her hands and knees on the oversized leather chair, grabbing the backrest. Lance slid inside of her, teasing her by pulling his hard rod in and out, as he rubbed the tip along the inside of her soaked lips. She gasped each time he went inside and pulled out.

"I need it now. Stop teasing me."

"Say it."

"Pump me baby. Give it to me now. I want you deep inside."

"I'm going to punish you. You've been a bad flight attendant."

"No!"

"Yes, you have!" as he pulled her hair. Lance pumped her faster as Candice excitement rose as she approached the climatic edge. The faster Lance slid inside of her, the louder Candice yelled. She was getting the ultimate thrill ride at 38,000 feet.

Seconds later, Candice yelled as she went over the orgasmic "cliff." Her legs jerked and quivered, as drops of sweat streamed down her face. Her neck was flushed pink with Lance's finger impressions. Candice intimate lips were soaked as her pleasure cave continued to throb from the epic aftershocks of her incredible eruption. The more she came, the tighter her pussy lips contracted around Lance's cock until he shoved all the way in her and came violently himself. Her passionate juices mixed with his continued, overflowing as it ran down her leg. Candice's breathing slowly returning to normal as she slumped into the chair.

"Welcome to the 'mile high' club", Lance whispered in her ear. She had earned her membership in the exclusive but erotic club. Her fantasies were no longer fantasies but relivable memories as she savored the moment. Candice wasn't sure what to do next. Although the perks of the job today exceed any previously challenging situations with demanding passengers, she realized she was working.

She regained her composure and awkwardly began straightening her clothes as she headed to the restroom. Once behind the door, she held onto the sink as she gazed into the mirror shaking her head in disbelief. Anxiety and self-consciousness overtook her thoughts as she evaluated the gravity of the situation. She "wrestled" with the fact that she just fucked a passenger. She always fantasized about having sex aboard an airplane but didn't consider the opportunity would be when she was supposed to be working. She took a cloth, washed her face, and cleaned up from her rendezvous. Candice took a deep breath as she prepared to face Lance.

Lance straightened his clothes and continued looking out the window as he reclined in his seat. He smiled to himself as he reflected on what had occurred. Although this was not his first sexual adventure on a plane, the experience with Candice was amazing. However, this adventure would eventually slip into the background of his memories. Lance was focused on his purpose in New York: to meet with Thomas Kent.

Candice face was still flushed as she closed the restroom door behind her. She immediately began preparing the inflight meal.

"Lance, would you like the baked chicken or pasta salad?" as she stood a couple feet away with her eyes downwardly casted.

Lance slowly turned his head to make eye contact and noticed her nervousness. He could feel her apprehension. "I will take the pasta salad."

Candice quickly turned to begin preparing the entree. As she walked to the galley, her eyes widened, chest rose and fell as she exhaled a deep breath. She quickly prepared his pasta salad; carrying the tray to his table.

"Lance, just as you requested. Bon Appetite!" as she gently set the tray on the table.

"Thank you." Lance quickly devoured his salad. He hadn't eaten since breakfast. Moments later, he rested the fork on the plate, gently pushing it away.

"Will there be anything else? Coffee?"

"You didn't offer me any dessert, as he paused. Lance

raised his finger, cocking his head to the side with a small wrinkle in his brow.

"I'm sorry. We have key lime pie or cheese cake." Candice said as she hurriedly walked toward the galley to get one of the selections.

"Wait!"

Candice turned around attentively listening to Lance's every word. "You gave me dessert earlier: the pink cookie with the cream filling" as he paused for a moment with his mouth opened before turning his expression into a smile.

Candice's face filled with redness as her eyes widened and rolled as she shook her head while placing her hands on her hips.

"What am I going to do with you? You are just too much. I don't know what to say."

"I do my best. Flight from LA to NYC: $5,000; in-flight meal-$50.00; the look on your face when asked about dessert: priceless," as Lance joined her in laughter.

"Why do you continue torturing me?"

"Embarrassing you yes; torturing you, never unless you are into that kinky sort of stuff", he grinned.

"Candice, no worries. Your secret is safe with me; I know how much you enjoy your career. I would never do anything to damage that for you. Besides, if I fly back to LA and you are available, I will request you personally."

Candice and Lance continued to laugh and talk for the remainder of the flight. She felt much better knowing her secret was safe. She enjoyed her time with Lance. He was fun in so many ways as she relished in her imaginative thoughts.

[Flight attendant; please prepare the cabin for landing].

"Lance, we will be landing soon. I will need for you to take your seat and fasten your seat belts."

"Yes ma'am. What will you have me do next? I am your sex slave", as he licked his tongue out holding his hands bent like two paws.

"You are clearly out of control. You need a spanking."

"I do. Will you promise to give me one if I continue to be bad?"

Lance gave Candice his card. "I know you get propositioned often, but remember who validated your membership into the 'mile high' club."

Lance's livery car picked him up from the airport and headed to his hotel. It was a 45-minute drive with minimal traffic. He enjoyed the moment of relaxation as a Frank Sinatra's song faintly played in the background. Lance reminisced and took this relaxing moment to reflect on how his life had changed. Seven years ago, his life was significantly different. He was a computer science student at Richard University for two years before he dropped out. He was bored and wanted to spend more time developing his application. He was either laser focused on a topic, or he couldn't concentrate on the task long enough to be effective. Lance was the only boy among his three sisters. At an early age, he showed an innate ability to figure things out. When he was 10, his great aunt gave him an old, broken record player that had been in the basement for years. Lance spent countless hours taking it apart in order to understand how the components worked or didn't work, and how he could repair it. He went to old thrift stores, garage sales, and novelty shops to get the needed parts. While other boys his age were playing sports or watching

TV, Lance was diligently working on the record player. He read magazines and searched the internet to discover all the information he could about the model and components. After many attempts, he continued to fail to get the record player working. He went back to the components and looked at multiple approaches. None of his approaches was effective. Although he failed dozens of times, Lance was focused and driven. When he failed, he would just start the process over by considering different options. He was determined to make the player work.

At school, Lance often asked his science teacher for help. Mr. Dennis was always helpful to students showing a keen interest in science and math. Significantly unpopular because of his slow speech and studious personality, many students teased Lance.

"Lance is a retard. Did your mommy drop you on your head when you were a baby? Lance you are just dumb."

"Stop saying those things. They are not true," Lance often replied when the kids called him bad names. Mr. Dennis often intervened when Lance became overwhelmed from the teasing.

"All students aren't the same nor do they learn at the same pace. However, teasing and ridiculing Lance doesn't make things better. Be respectful to your classmate."

After six months, Lance called his aunt to tell her he had a surprise for her.

"Aunt Joan, this is Lance. Can you come over to the house?"

"Yes, what is it?"

"I have a surprise for you."

"What is it?"

"You got to come over to the house. I will show you", as he tapped on the table.

"Ok, I will be over shortly." Aunt Joan put on her slippers and walked down the block. She only lived a couple blocks away.

"What is it Lance?"

Lance grabbed her hand and led her down to the basement.

Full of excitement-"Cover her eyes".

"Ok."

Lance uncovered the sheet to reveal the old record player. He had cleaned and repaired it.

"Listen to this Aunt Joan", as he carefully placed a vinyl record on top; gently releasing the lever to place the needle on the record. A couple seconds of hissing and out of the speakers came the sultry voice of Frank Sinatra.

Aunt Joan closed her eyes momentarily and smiled as she looked over at Lance. "You are truly special and gifted.

"Thank you Aunt Joan. I just wanted to see why you made such a big deal about the player. It does sound good. I wanted to make you happy."

"You have truly done that. I didn't know you planned on fixing the record player when I gave it to you. It hasn't worked in years. I've been meaning to throw it out, but I just didn't get around to it. I'm glad I didn't know."

"Now you can enjoy it Aunt Joan. I will bring it back over to the house this coming weekend." Lance was proud to have repaired the old player. He saw the satisfaction on Aunt Joan's face.

Lance eventually overcame his speech impediment and went on to be a stellar student. Throughout high school, he continued to explore the many facets of science and computers. Often spending extensive hours in the computer lab, Lance learned several programming languages, including C++, C#, Java Script, SQL and Python. He still struggled in social settings. There were a few girls he liked, but often said inappropriate things to them. Joe McGee was a year older than Lance. Joe loved football but struggled in chemistry and math classes.

"Hey Lance, right?"

"Yeah!"

"I'm Joe. I'm struggling in math. Can you help me out man?"

"I'm not going to do your homework."

"Nah! I really do need some help. Can you like, tutor so I can at least pass? I ain't no scholar or nothing like that. I just need to pass, so I can play football."

"What's in it for me?"

"Maybe I won't beat you up. I'm just joking. I see you ain't real popular with the girls. Me, on the other hand, I'm smooth. You like Carol, right?"

"How do you know that?"

"Man everybody knows that. Where you been? I can help ya out", slumping down in his chair. "I got swag, and I can hook you up—deal?"

"Deal."

Lance helped Joe pass algebra II, and Joe helped him with approaching girls. After some coaching, Joe introduced Lance to Carol. Things started a little rough. After more coaching, Lance became a natural at approaching girls. He learned a lot from Joe.

He approached Carol again. Perhaps this time he would fare better than before.

"Hi Carol."

"Hi Lance."

"Sorry about sneezing on you last time. I get nervous and it causes me to sneeze sometimes."

"It's ok. Things happen."

"The school dance is Friday. Would you like to go with me? We can grab an ice cream before the dance." Lance said casually.

"I would like that."

"Cool. I will give you a call Thursday to confirm a time."

"Ok. That sounds good", as she smiled and twirled her hair. Things did go well. This was Lance's turning point with girls. Joe's coaching had paid off. He no longer stumbled for words. Lance became a natural conversationalist.

"Mr. Howard, we will be arriving at your hotel in 5 minutes."

"Thank you."

Lance checked in and headed up to his presidential suite. It was 1300 square feet of pure luxury and comfort. He tipped the bellhop and sat down in the oversized chair. His day had been nonstop since 7am West coast time. It was after midnight and he was just getting settled into his commodious accommodations. He smiled to himself and took a moment to reflect on his thrilling flight from Los Angeles. Candice definitely made his trip memorable. He ordered room service and retired for the night.

Beep! Beep! Beep! Lance's alarm went off at 6am faithfully every morning. Lance rolled over, gently stuck his hands from underneath the covers to hit the snooze button. Nine minutes later, the alarm went off again. Lance sighed, groaned, and pulled the covers from over his head. It was time to get up. He turned his feet and sat on the bed, wiped his eyes, and took a deep breath.

Lance rose to his feet, went to the bathroom, and threw water on his face. He went to the kitchen to pour a large glass of water. It was time to hydrate before his workout. Lance dressed and went down to the hotel fitness center to get his workout started.

After his workout, he ordered room service: three egg whites, 3 slices of tomatoes, chicken breast and a glass of orange juice. He jumped in the shower before his breakfast arrived.

* * *

[Phone Rang]

"Hello."

"Hey Lance, this is Joe McGee."

"Hey Joe!"

"I was just giving you a call. I know you just flew in last night. How was your flight?"

"It was great. It was a bumpy flight but everything smoothed out eventually."

"Was that the plane or the hot one you were doing on the flight?"

"Both! You know me too well."

"We go back so far. What was it, high school before I graduated and moved to the East coast?"

"I think so. How have you been man?"

"I've been good. It's been a busy time for me, but when I got your call a few weeks ago, I was surprised, but glad I could help."

"I am too. I will fill you in on the details when we see each other in a couple of hours.

"Are you ready for the meeting with Thomas Kent? I have already set things up and gave him a brief overview. I didn't want to 'steal your thunder,' so I didn't give him many details."

"I appreciate it. I can give him my full blown pitch and see where it goes."

"That sounds good. Do you want to meet 30 minutes before the meeting so we can catch up and go over a few things?'"

"That sounds like a winner. I will see you in an hour and a half."

The three men scheduled meeting was for 10:30am at the Wintergreen Country Club. The club was exclusive members only with special guest invitation privileges. Joe often met at the club to negotiate key deals and contracts. The location was quiet, relaxed, but conducive for a business setting. Since Thomas also was a member, Joe wanted to meet him in familiar surroundings.

Lance and Joe arrived about the same time. Lance had the driver drop him off at the entrance. Joe arrived in his black M5 BMW coupe. The two men saw each other in the parking lot.

"Joe, how are you doing man", as Lance firmly shook his hand and patting him on the back.

"I'm great. It's so good to see you again as well. It's been way too long."

"I know. Where are we meeting?"

"Come on, I will show you. Have you eaten yet?"

"I ate breakfast earlier, but I never turn down good food", Lance grinned.

The two friends visited the buffet, got some food, and relaxed on the veranda overlooking the greens. They took this opportunity to catch up before the formal meeting with Kent.

"I still can't believe how well things have worked out for you. I remember back in high school when you were struggling in math and now look at you. You are a top sports agent with a long list of successful clients. I'm impressed."

"I still haven't used that algebra but I did gain valuable insight in statistics. I am constantly reviewing clients' stats in order to negotiate the best contract for them", as he cracked a smile.

"I see you don't have any challenges with women these days. I also remembered you sneezed on that girl you liked. What was her name, Carol?"

"Yes, her name was Carol", he smiled.

"After all my coaching and an introduction, you 'fumbled the ball.'"

"Well, I may have 'fumbled the ball,' but I still scored a touchdown; a few of them actually," as Lance winked and pointed to Joe. They both laughed.

"When are you getting married Joe?"

"How about the day before never," the two of them chuckled. "I'm having too much fun without the headaches. With my salary, I can rent a lot of cows and get the milk at a discount."

"Joe, you are out of control."

"Well, what can I say?"

"What about you, Lance? Since you are young, hot, and successful, I'm sure you get your share of imposed proposals."

"Joe, you wouldn't believe the number of women that assertively approach me. After my company went public, the 'floodgates' of women opened and the 'flash flood' of sexual incentives continued with no slowdowns in sight. It's just crazy."

"Lance, I can only imagine. After I get a big contract for my clients, women flock to them like the changing of the seasons."

"Enough about our current and future conquests, tell me a little about Thomas Kent. I know you set up the meeting."

"I met Thomas Kent at one of the NFL's owners' conferences. He is a smooth-talking charismatic businessman. Thomas is in his early sixties. He is a self-made multi-millionaire with an estimated net worth of about 800 million."

"How did he make his money?"

"He was a sports agent/attorney and eventually bought a minority ownership in one of the local NFL teams.

Thomas Kent arrived wearing a button down shirt, business casual blazer, and blue slacks. Thomas was a clean-shaven gentleman with salt and pepper colored hair on the side. He looked anything but his age of sixty-one.

Joe and Lance both stood when Thomas arrived at the table. Joe introduced Lance to Thomas Kent.

"Mr. Kent, I'm Lance Howard", Lance extended his hand to give him a firm handshake.

"Lance, call me Thomas. I see enough of that during the workweek."

"Thank you."

"So where did you meet Joe?"

"Joe and I went to high school together. He was a year ahead of me, but our paths crossed.

"Lance helped me with math back in school", Joe chimed.

"Obviously his assistance paid off."

"So tell me more about this meeting." Thomas wasted no time getting down to business.

"A little bit about me. I'm an application developer working out of San Jose, California. I have been in the software development business for about eight years now, and I successful took my start-up business public three years ago. I would like to leverage my success in software development to the real estate business by purchasing land and building a soccer stadium in the Washington DC area. I am seeking investors to form a joint venture to purchase land, build a stadium, and establish a soccer franchise team in the DC area. Does that sound like something that may interest you?"

"Lance thank you for your overview." Thomas sat back in his chair and crossed his fingers. He paused for a moment as he cocked his head to the side with eyes slightly turned upward. Thomas then rubbed his chin.

"You know I have some questions for you", as Thomas finally broke his silence.

"I expected as much. I know you are a prudent business-man and wouldn't be where you are today if you weren't."

Joe sat back and crossed his fingers—watching the two men exchange information. He found the exchange intriguing as two competing alpha males 'locking horns' over the last morsel of food.

"How much are you projecting the stadium will cost? The franchise? What will be your role in the partnering group? How many investors do you have onboard already?

How much are you prepared to put into the deal to make it work?"

"Thomas, those are all good questions. I have preliminary numbers for the stadium cost at $480 million; my role is to lead the project to include marketing and business development; I am putting $100 million of my money into the deal; and you would be the first investor," Lance replied.

"Lance, I admire your commitment and passion to make things happen. You live in San Jose but how are you supposed to manage a project on the other end of the country? In addition, do you have any politicians in your 'pocket'? You are going to need them to get legislation passed in favor of your initiative. Another thing, who do you know on the ground in DC that can put this kind of deal together?"

"No, I don't have any connections with politicians in DC. I didn't think I needed any to make the deal happen. I am working my contacts to locate an architectural firm that can handle this scope of operation," Lance replied hesitatively.

"I'm sorry Lance but there are too many unknowns and unanswered questions. I don't feel comfortable investing at this time. If there were other investors and a solid team in place for the land development portion, I would be willing to take a chance."

"Thank you Thomas for your time", as Lance and Joe stood up to leave the table.

"Wait. What I can do for you is help you with part of the unknowns. Have you hear of Monica Salazar?"

"No, I don't know her."

"She is the power player in the DC area. If anyone knows the 'lay of the land', that person would be Monica. I can set up an introduction. Besides, if you are going to run a project in DC, you might want to buy a house in the area so you can learn the 'players' in the market."

"I really appreciate your help."

"Don't mention it. I like to see young people succeed." Thomas nodded as his espresso arrived.

Lance came to the painful truth and reality that he had a lot of "homework" to do to get his soccer stadium proposal off the ground. He didn't have any political contacts, connections, or a good starting point. He wasn't familiar with the real estate business let alone the sports franchise side of the business. Lance had a lot of hurdles to overcome in this effort for anyone to consider. He was out of his league but still needed these same power players as part of the overall "equation".

The good news was that Thomas felt empathetic toward Lance's efforts to make the deal possible. Thomas was at least interested but wasn't willing to be the "token guinea pig" of investors. Lance had a lot of "ground" to cover. His first starting point was Monica Salazar.

* * *

Lance and Joe lingered around in the parking lot to have a personal conversation. Lance had a lot of work to do.

"Joe, what did you think about that meeting?"

"Well, I think Thomas is a smart guy and he gave you a lot of good insight on a way forward."

"Right! I just got my ass handed to me", as Lance shrugged and shook his head.

"Well, I didn't want to say it but that is pretty much what I saw. However, Thomas is a fair businessman, and he likes to see people succeed but he's not going to give it to you. You have to earn it."

I may be down but that doesn't mean I'm out. I will have to look at things differently and take a different approach. The good news is that Thomas gave me a contact. Do you know Monica?"

"I've never heard of her but that doesn't mean much. Remember I'm in the sport agency business. I don't know much about real estate let alone in DC. It's worth a shot to see where the lead takes you. I will get with Thomas's assistant to get the contact information and coordinate a time when he can give her a call. You are going to owe me big time."

Man, don't I know it. You can always put it on my running tab." Lance smiled while Joe nodded and winked.

A couple weeks later, Joe set up the video conference call with Thomas, Monica, and Lance. Although Joe didn't have a stake in the deal, he continued to help Lance put the meeting together.

[Video Conference Call]

"Hello Monica,"

"Hello Thomas, it's been a long time. How are things going?"

"Things are going well on my end. I want to introduce you to a young up and coming entrepreneur who is looking at doing some business in the DC area. I will let him tell you a little more about himself. Lance, this is Monica Salazar"

"Thank you Thomas for facilitating this introduction. Monica, My name is Lance Howard. It is a pleasure to meet you. As Thomas said, I'm interested in putting together a business proposal and your name was at the top of the list of people that make things happen. I look forward to meeting you in person. I wanted this to be a brief introduction and I will coordinate with your assistant to get on your calendar to meet in person to discuss."

"That sounds good."

"Again, Thomas, I appreciate you setting up this introduction."

"No problem Lance. I'm glad I can help."

All parties disconnected from the call. Although it was a short call, Lance felt the call was very productive. Monica now at least had a face with the name which will facilitate a better in person meeting.

Lance called Joe to follow-up from the meeting.

"Hey Lance, how did the teleconference go with Monica and Thomas?"

"Better than expected. I was surprised but it was only an introduction. Thomas provided a good Segway into getting to know Monica. I look forward to meeting her in person. It should be interesting."

"Lance, that sounds excellent. So how does she look? I mean, is she a hag?"

"Oh no! To be honest, she is hot."

"What she look like on a scale of 1 to 10?"

"I would give her about an eight."

"Wow. That is high in your book. I'm surprised. You don't usually get excited about much when it comes to women. I guess Monica is the exception right?"

"Oh yes. I wouldn't kick her out of bed, unless I could do her on the floor."

"Oh she is doable?"

"Very much so. She is a little older than what I normally prefer, but I'm open to expanding my horizons", Lance grinned.

"You still haven't told me what she look like. Why you holding out on me man?"

"I'm sorry. She is slender build, well dressed with medium length brown hair. She looks like she is Venezuelan or Brazilian. I'm not sure. From what I can see, she looks like she is in her early to mid-forties."

"Sounds nice. I can always live vicariously through you."

"Joe, you really need to stop. This is about business."

"Are you telling me you wouldn't do her if you had a chance?"

"In a heartbeat. Are you kidding", Lance laughed.

"Well, I will let you know more. I'm scheduled to meet Monica in person next week. That will give me some time to learn about "cougars" without the long tails."

"As usual, you are out of control."

CHAPTER 2

L ANCE prepared to meet with Monica. He flew back to San Jose shortly after the meeting with Thomas. He had a lot of things to do and some tough decisions to make. He thought about the things Thomas told him. Lance needed to be on the ground to lead this venture. He couldn't effectively do that from California. Lance decided to purchase a house in the Washington DC area. He wanted to be local to be able to interact with the key players and build relationships. Purchasing a home would also give Monica an incentive to be more receptive to building a business. Besides, he would have an opportunity to interact with Monica. Lance was looking forward to seeing her in person. As he prepared to head back to the East Coast, he thought about Candice.

[Phone Rang] Candice picked up the phone to answer.

"Hello Candice, how are you."

"I'm doing well. May I ask who is calling?"

"This is Lance or like you often said, 'Mr. Howard.'"

"Oh hey! How are you doing? I didn't recognize the number but since few people call me, I thought it might be someone that knows me. I see I was right", as she smiled to herself.

"You are a smart woman. I noticed that on the plane. I know you didn't think I would ever call you.

"You are correct; now you are the smart guy on the phone", as she sighed.

"Things have been busy for me lately. I was in NY on business when we met, but I'm back on the West Coast. How have things been going in your world? Have you been to any interesting places?"

"No, I haven't had much excitement. I have just been flying as usual."

"Now that you have had time to think, what did you think about your introduction to the 'mile high' club?"

Candice paused for a moment. "It was interesting to say the least. I have never done anything like that before, but there is a first time for everything", as she smiled and twirled her hair.

"I'm sure you are probably a frequent flyer in the club, and I was just a connecting 'flight' along the way", as her face frowned with a wrinkle in her brow.

"No, it's not like that at all. To be honest, I have only done that two other times. Getting intimate on a plane is not my style. It was a spontaneous situation that occurred."

"I see. So did you call either of the other two women?"

"No, I didn't."

"So why are you calling me?" Candice curiosity was running wild. She didn't know what to think. Was he being honest? Is he trying to hook up with me again? Is he really interested in me? Candice wasn't sure what Lance's motivation was. She did realize that he called her.

"I called you because we connected on more than just a physical level. You sparked my interest, and I would like to get to know you better. I don't think a four-hour flight is long enough to get to know someone even if it does involves sex. Besides, I would like to take you to dinner."

Candice paused. Her thoughts went back to her time with Lance on the plane. As she rubbed the nape of her neck, she thought about how he breathed on the back of her neck as he stood behind her. She reminisced about Lance's strong hands all over her body. Candice also imagined what it would be like to see Lance again.

"So are you asking me out?"

"Yes!" as he smiled and flipped a pen between his fingers.

"Well let me think about it."

"Oh, ok", as Lance eyes rolled and his head leaned back to look at the phone. "Give me a call later and let me know what you decided", as he politely but casually ended the call. Lance was somewhat surprised.

Candice exercised all of her remaining self-control in speaking with Lance. Lance's deep voice gave Candice a sizzling and tingly sensation. She could feel him in her mind. However, she had to remain calm. Although her body was yearning for his touch, she couldn't let Lance possess control over her emotions and have free reins with her feelings. Candice stalled. I will let him wait.

Lance shrugged off Candice's coolness in her response to his invitation. Although he wanted to see her, he had other things that required his focus and attention. After his meeting with Thomas, Lance was decisively engaged in the business at hand. This meeting with Monica is an excellent opportunity to form a critical business relationship in DC.

[Phone Rang]

"Hello!"

"This is Candice. I accept your invitation. It will be nice to see you again."

"I look forward to seeing you again as well. I know it's only been a month but it will be nice to sit down in a relaxed environment and just talk."

"That sounds good. I will be in LA next week. What day and time is good for you?"

Lance took a quick flight down from San Jose to Los Angeles. After arriving, a driver picked him up from the airport. Lance had a meeting scheduled with another investor: Sebastian Cross. Sebastian Cross was a real estate mogul on the West Coast primarily in commercial office buildings. Sabastian was always looking for a new opportunity to expand his empire of over 2 million square feet in leased office space. Although eccentric in his personal life, Sebastian was a shrewd businessman when it came to real estate deals. He was a burly man with a receding hairline. He has been married and divorced twice. He drank regularly and smoked a cigar.

Lance met Sebastian at The Athenaeum in Pasadena on a Friday afternoon. The weather was unseasonably mild, usual for Southern California.

"Mr. Cross, thank you for taking the time to meet me."

"Call me Sebastian! Mr. Cross is for people I don't know and probably don't want to know", as he gave a heavy chuckle which turned into a nasty cough.

"Where are you from Lance?"

"I'm from New York, but I spent the last few years in San Jose. I guess I'm from New York. What about you?"

"I'm from San Francisco, but I have spent the last 30

years in LA. So I guess I'm a Californian. We all travel and move around in life, so wherever people spend most of their time, is where they should call home. There are a few exceptions. Do you travel back to New York? Do you still have family there? Parents?" as Sebastian sat back in his chair sipping his cognac.

"Yes, I get back a few times a year. My parents are in their early sixties, but they both are still active. They travel, volunteer, and keep busy. Why do you ask—I'm curious?" Lance leaned back in his chair with his hands resting across his chair.

"I like to know a little about the person I may be doing business with in the future. I like to know where he or she comes from and how he/she got to where they are now. I want to know where they consider home and a little about their relationship with their parents."

"Did I answer all your questions?"

"Yes, I have a pretty good insight at this point. So tell me about your proposal. I know my friend Daniel Williams referred me to you and set up this meeting."

"Daniel Williams?"

"Dan is friends with Henry Howard, the chairman of the board of your company."

"I see, interesting."

"Lance, in business, it's not who you know, but who knows you. So, let's hear your pitch."

Lance took a deep breath and began his proposal.

"Thank you again Mr. Cross for taking the time to meet with me."

"Call me Sebastian", as he nodded his head.

"Sebastian, my proposal is to purchase land and build

a soccer stadium in the Washington DC area. The market is prime to support a soccer stadium with the demographics, and income. There was a preliminary proposal a couple of years ago but the developer couldn't raise adequate capital to fund the project and sustain the franchise. The initial estimates for the land and construction are $480 million with an additional $200 million in payroll and operations budget for the first two years of the franchise. After that, the franchise should be cash positive. I will be the lead investor with my $100 million equity overseeing the project from DC. I have contacted a real estate brokerage firm that has the capacity and network to undertake a project of this magnitude. I am seeking investors for a joint venture to own the land, stadium and soccer team franchise in the DC area. Does that sound like something of interest to you?"

"Lance, sounds like you have done some homework. What is the projected return on investment and timeline?

"With the land, my team estimated a capitalization rate of 12 percent. From a franchising perspective, payroll would be high in the first two years of operations but the trend would have a downward vector as personnel and athletes come under contract. The projected return on investment is 8 percent after year two in my financial model after the completion of construction."

"Lance, I'm going to take a chance with you and see where this deal goes. Send the financials over to my office on Monday and I will have my executive team review the numbers. If they make sense like the ones we discussed, I will be in for $100 million as well. Besides, since I'm not going to live forever, I am going to live on the 'edge' from time to time", as he puffed on his Cuba cigar, and coughed.

"Sebastian, I want to thank you for the opportunity. I will send those financials over to your team on Monday", as both men rose from their seats, shook hands, and Lance left the table.

Lance focused intensely to maintain his poise throughout the meeting. After Sebastian expressed interest in investing in the project, Lance could barely contain his excitement. He was relieved that Sebastian didn't ask how many other investors were onboard with the project. Lance had learned a lot since his first meeting with Thomas Kent, which was a disaster. Lance was on the move with his project finally gaining traction toward 'getting off the ground.'"

[Phone Rang]

"Hello!"

"Lance, how are things going? Are you in town now?"

"Yes, you have excellent timing. I just finished a meeting with a key prospective investor and he agreed to come onboard provided my numbers make sense."

"That is excellent. That calls for a celebration."

"For sure. Does tomorrow night work for you?"

"Yes, that would be great."

"I look forward to seeing you again. It's been too long, so I want to take you somewhere nice."

"I would really like that a lot," she responded while twirling her hair. "I will speak with you soon."

[Phone rings]

"Hey Jennifer, what's up?"

"Hey Candice, what are you doing tomorrow? It's been a minute since we got together and had some girl time. We need to get out and catch up."

"I would love to but not tomorrow. I have a date."

"So who are you trading a girl's night on the town in for?"

"His name is Lance."

"Lance who?"

"Lance Howard. Why so many questions?"

"I'm just asking. No need to get your panties in a knot. Tell me about this Lance guy. What does he do for a living? Girl, I want all the details", as Jennifer laughed.

"If you must know, he is a software application developer out of San Jose, and he is in town this weekend."

"Oh, I see. Wait! He wouldn't be Lance Howard, the founder of the PicApp would he?"

"I'm not sure. He told me he develops apps for sharing videos and pictures."

"Oh my God!"

"It's the same guy. Candice, he is loaded. He took his company public a few years ago and his estimated net worth is about $300 million. He is not bad on the eyes at all. I would fuck him."

"Jen, you are just scandalous. You are clearly out of control", she shook her head.

"Where did you meet him?"

"I met him on a flight I was working on heading to New York."

"See, some people have all the luck. I meet washed up losers. I knew I should have been a flight attendant, but I couldn't take all that flying. Is he nice? You know some guys are arrogant pricks in real life."

"No, he has good social skills for a geek. I was surprised. He didn't talk about work nor himself. Actually, he has a droll personality."

"Oh really. That's really good to know. I will stop "grilling" you with questions. You know I want to know all the details from the date later this weekend."

"I will see what I can do," Candice responded in a noncommittal tone.

"Don't do anything I wouldn't do! Wait, I might not be a good example in this situation." Jen cachinnated for effect.

"Uh huh! It's all good." Candice wouldn't dare tell Jennifer she had already had sex with Lance especially when she was supposed to be working. It would be her little secret for now.

* * *

Lance's driver arrived at Candice's apartment. Lance got out and went to the main entrance as he called her cell phone.

"Candice, I'm in the lobby."

"I will be right down."

"Ok, I will see you shortly." Lance knew she wouldn't be right down. It's the nature of a woman to take longer than advertised. He was fine waiting. Things were going well. He had tentatively gotten his first investor onboard, and he would be flying to DC to meet Monica in less than two weeks. Things were slowly falling into place.

Lance checked his watch, looked in the nearby mirror, and adjusted his hair and shirt. Lance dressed more like a nightclub owner than a software developer did. With designer shirts and tailored suits, Lance was not your stereotypical nerd. Although he loved technology and always has, he was often characterized as a maverick after the launch of his software company. However, if Lance had an avatar, it would be a playboy. This self-perspective showed in the way he dressed.

As Lance turned around, the elevator door opened and Candice stepped out wearing three-inch open toed heels, a sleeveless sheer midnight blue dress that hugged her curvaceous figure, a silk scarf around her neck, and a dainty bracelet. Candice' painted nails matched her painted toes perfectly. Her ebony hair rested on her shoulders; neutral blush accented her cheeks; and her eyeliner accentuated her long natural eyelashes.

Lance mouth fell open, leaving him speechless. He had never seen Candice look this stunning. He was in awe and amazed. Lance walked toward her to give her a warm but gentle embrace as a couple of Candice's neighbors waved as she greeted Lance.

"Hi Candice, it's really good to see you again." Lance eyes widened.

"It's good to see you as well", as her eyes gazed upon him. She instantaneously replayed the episode on the plane as she smiled.

"You look lovely." Lance replied.

"I have been known to clean up well. You just thought my wardrobe was only a flight attendant outfit didn't you?"

"You got me", as they both laughed.

They arrived at the Raymond, the most exclusive restaurant in the San Gabriel Valley. The driver dropped them off right at the main entrance.

The host quickly greeted Lance and Candice.

Mr. Howard, your reservation is in order; right this way. Candice was surprised at the prompt service.

"When I grow up, I want to be just like you." Candice mentioned.

"What do you mean?"

"I mean that you receive celebrity caliber service usually associated with a movie star or a star athlete." I have heard that this restaurant only takes reservations, and is always booked on the weekends."

"I may know a few key people. It does pay to have a few dollars in place", Lance laughed.

"I can imagine."

They were having a relaxing dinner until Lance's phone rang.

"Are you going to answer that call?"

"Excuse me one moment. This is Lance. Hello, Sebastian, I'm surprised to get your call. What time? 9 am. Will this meeting be at the same private club? Ok, I will see you there. Talk to you soon."

"Is everything Ok," Candice asked.

"I have a meeting with Sebastian and one of his business partners in the morning. I don't know what it's about, but this is not a good sign receiving a call late on a Friday night from my first investor."

"You don't know that. It could be something positive. You have to keep an open mind."

"I been in business long enough to know that late night phone calls are usually not good signs, especially from a new investor. I wonder if he has changed his mind. It doesn't make sense to meet another business partner. Maybe Sebastian wants me to pitch the concept to him and his business partner to make sure they both didn't miss anything."

"Well, you will know tomorrow. I'm sure you will be prepared for a presentation if needed. You convinced me to get naked on a plane."

Lance laughed. "You are right. That was a wild time, but I enjoyed it."

"I did as well. It was fun, exciting and adventurous; not to mention risky," as Candice twirled her hair. "I still can't believe I did that at work."

"A toast to occupational perks", as they both laughed. The couple continued small talk as they enjoyed the restaurant ambience. There was smooth jazz playing in the background.

"Would you like dessert?" Lance inquired before their waiter returned.

"I'm thinking about the key lime pie. What about you; what are you thinking of for dessert?" as she reviewed the menu.

"I'm thinking about the juicy cookie with the cream filling from the airplane", he jokingly smirked as Candice hit him on the arm.

"That is just wrong," she responded, shaking her head. "You will have no cookie tonight. You have an early day tomorrow", waving her finger from side to side.

* * *

Lance got up early the next morning to go over the specifics of his presentation. He was looking at various worst-case scenarios as a contingency in case Sebastian wanted to pull out of the deal. What will I do if his business partner is not onboard? What will I do if his business partner hates the deal and sways Sebastian to walk away from the deal? All these thoughts clouded Lance's mind as he reviewed each detail of his proposal.

Lance arrived at Annandale Golf Club early to review

the presentation. Every detail had to be on point. He had worked hard to get Sebastian onboard, and he wasn't about to lose any ground. If so, he would start all over working to get his first investor onboard.

The two men approached the table where Lance was sitting. Lance rose to greet both men.

"Lance, I appreciate you meeting us on such short notice. I would like to introduce you to Jonathan Westin. Jonathan is a venture capitalist I have done business with in the past, and I wanted him to hear your pitch."

"Sure, that is not a problem at all. If we can get the standard non-disclosure agreement formality out of the way, I can jump right into the presentation."

"NDA, why would I sign a NDA to just hear a pitch. It's not like I'm reviewing your financials and marketing plan." Jon sharply remarked.

"I understand your hesitation, and I'm sure you hear presentations and pitches on a regular basis. However, as a prudent businessperson, NDAs are standard protocol to maintain intellectual property integrity. I hope you will understand."

"I usually don't sign a NDA for an initial pitch, but I will make an exception because Sabastian had favorable things to say." Jon frowned while reluctantly signing the paper.

Lance proceeded with his thirty-minute pitch covering the overview, the marketing strategy, financial projections and investment targets. His presentation was on point. Sebastian smiled with raised eyebrows with a partial smile as Lance covered areas not previously mentioned during the presentation with him. Sebastian scribbled notes when Lance covered unfamiliar points.

However, Jon maintained a cold callous demeanor showing no emotions or responses to any points Lance made. Jon's breathing was even as he sat back in his chair with his legs crossed resting his hands on his lap. His eyes narrowed as he watched Lance's body language throughout the presentation. After about ten minutes, he shifted his legs down on the floor and positioned his curled hand under his chin cocking his head slightly to the left.

"Lance you made some insightful points. Send my team the financials and a prospectus and if I have any additional questions, I will be in touch. I apologize for my abrupt departure, but I have another engagement to attend." Jon replied.

"Mr. Westin, I thank you for taking time out of your busy schedule", as Lance firmly shook his hand and then Sebastian's hand.

"Call me Jon", as the two men departed.

Lance exhaled a big sigh of relief after the two men departed the building. He couldn't believe what had just happened. He wasn't sure if Jon was onboard or insulted. However, the bright side of the overall meeting was that Sebastian was totally onboard with the venture; Jon, perhaps not so much. Lance ordered lunch and enjoyed the small victory.

[Phone Rang]

"Hello."

"Lance, this is Joe McGee."

"Joe, I know it's you. I have you in my phone contacts. What's going on with you?"

"I wanted to reach out to see how things were going. I know we haven't spoken in a while."

"It's been interesting to say the least. I got commitment

from my first investor since we've spoken and a business associated introduced me to a venture capitalist. He is a real stone-faced emotionless guy. His name is Jonathan Westin. Do you know him?"

"I don't know him, but I have heard of him. He is a no nonsense kind of guy to put it mildly. He may not be friendly, but he is a good businessperson to know. He has been a venture capitalist for about 15 years. He helped Pearson Caldwell grow his business and took it public."

"Is Pearson the same person that developed software to data mine and consolidated patient records on mobile devices?"

"Yep!"

"I read about him."

"Jon put the IPO together and the two of them made tens of millions. He has the connections to many high net worth individuals. Like I said, he is a good person to know."

"He seems like a prick."

"Maybe so but he is a wealthy prick, and he knows other wealthy pricks," as the two men laughed.

Jon and Sebastian walked to their awaiting car. Once inside the car, the two men had a private conversation.

"Sebastian, you think he bought it?"

"Why not, he doesn't suspect anything. He believes I'm a legitimate investor that is interested in his project. Besides, $100 million is a small price to pay when billions are on the line. We will see how this plays out. In the meantime, we will continue with the plan."

"Sebastian, I knew I could count on you to find me the next big deal. Remember, you owe me and I always collect", as both men laughed.

CHAPTER 3

LANCE calls Jonathan a couple weeks later to follow-up on the information from their meeting. Lance already had one investor but needs others to build legitimacy for his epic business venture.

"Hello Jon, how are things going?"

"Things are going well. I have several projects going simultaneously; normal business activities for me. What's up?"

"I wanted to follow-up to see if you have reviewed the information from our meeting a couple weeks ago?"

"Actually I briefly reviewed the information on my flight back to Chicago. I have some things I would like to discuss with you. Can you come to Chicago next week?"

"Let me check my schedule, but I believe I should be able to fly out there. How does Thursday of next week look for you?"

"Thursday may be good. Just reach out to my personal assistant to set things up."

"That sounds good. I look forward to meeting with you again."

Lance made flight reservation for his Chicago trip. He was surprised that Jon reviewed his prospectus. As he sat at his desk reviewing his calendar, he remembered he needed to reconnect with Monica and schedule a meeting with her.

[Salazar Realty, how may I direct your call?]

"Monica Salazar, Please."

"May I ask who is calling?"

"Yes, tell her it is Lance Howard. We had a video conference call about three weeks ago with Thomas Kent."

"Lance, it's good to speak with you again. How are things going?"

"Things are going well. I am working feverously to align investors for my upcoming project. The purpose of my call is to schedule a meeting to discuss more details of my prospectus. What is your available the week of 22nd of next month?"

"Let me check with my assistant and get back with you. That week may be ok but I want to make sure."

"That is fair enough. I look forward to hearing from you soon. By the way, I'm doing some preliminary research for places to live in the DC area. Do you have any neighborhoods you would recommend?"

"In Maryland, I would recommend Bethesda or Potomac; in DC, Georgetown; and in Virginia, I would recommend Mclean. Those are just a few but we can talk about it more in person."

"Thanks for the recommendations. I will follow up with you soon."

[Monica has a nice voice. She sounds friendly but sophisticated. I wonder if she is married. Maybe, she isn't interested in a younger man. I'm sure she is always interested in business. Lance, get a hold of yourself. What am I thinking? This is supposed to be about business. Well I guess thoughts never harm anyone.]

* * *

Lance's private jet flight arrived in Chicago Wednesday night with a driver picking him up curbside. The driver took him to his hotel located in the downtown area.

"Mr. Howard, the drive is going to be about 45 minutes. Would you like to stop anywhere?"

"No, I'm fine thank you."

Lance's hotel was in the downtown area off East Walton Street. Lance reviewed his presentation for possible scenario questions Jon may ask. What information is not in the prospectus? Is he really interested in investing in the project? Is this guy jerking me around?

Lance checked into his capacious hotel suite of 1248 square feet. It offered all the comforts of home, and then some: A furnished outdoor terrace, fireplace, separate bedroom with king-sized bed, elegant living room with a dining table and queen-sized sofa bed, full master bath with a soaking tub, as well as a separate powder room. Other features included complimentary Wi-Fi access, two 42-inch LCD HDTVs with DVR, virtual surround system with iPod integration and wet bar including refrigerator, freezer, and microwave. Lance booked a suite that offered city views. He often booked luxury accommodation when he traveled. A relaxing environment creates comfort and takes away from the stress associated with the constant travel.

Lance arrived at Jonathan's office around 10:30am for his 11:00 o'clock meeting. An early reconnoiter allowed him to locate the office before his important meeting.

Jon came to the reception area to meet Lance.

"Hey Lance, glad you could make it. I see you made it

here with no difficulties. How was your flight," as the two men walked into Jon's office.

"I left a little early just to be sure. My charter flight was great. Traffic wasn't bad when I arrived last night."

"Where are you staying?"

"I'm at the King Suites off of Walton Street."

"I know that place. I haven't stayed there, but I have heard nothing but good things about it."

"It's a pretty nice spot. So you mentioned on the phone that you had some questions about my financials. What specific questions did you have? Perhaps I can clarify."

"You mentioned you were interested in purchasing land, building a stadium, and establishing a team franchise. Is that correct?"

"Yes, I plan to take a three prong approach to establishing a brand. The demographics support a team and the nearest team to DC is out of New York."

"Do you have projections broken out for each venture or did you consolidate the numbers?" as Jon glanced at the financial on his mahogany desk. What are the long term projections: 10 or 15 years?"

"I consolidated the numbers based on a 10-year model."

"Lance, let me be frank with you. If you want to get a better response with investors, I would recommend you break each venture out separately. Secondly, this venture is outside of my area of focus, so I wouldn't be interested in investing."

[Lance took a deep breath; eyes narrowed, and face tightened as he took all the information in from the meeting. I can't believe I traveled here for these minor questions. He isn't even interested in investing. Why did he have me come all the way out here to waste my time? He is such a prick. If I didn't need his money or connections, I would tell him to fuck himself. However, my friend Joe had a valid point. Jon and his associates are good people to know, and it's all part of the business.]

"Jon, I understand and will take your recommendations into consideration."

"Lance, all is not lost. I do know a business associate that may be interested in your sports venture. I will give him a call and see if he is available for a meeting. I can't make any promises because he is extremely busy. When do you fly back?"

"I was going to fly back on Friday morning. Why?"

"Let me make some calls and see if any of my contacts are interested in buying into your venture. If you don't have any pressing events, I can show you around Chicago and introduce you to a couple of people while you are in town."

"Jon, I can push my departure time back to late tomorrow evening. Just give me a call later, and we can go from there. I will get my people started on making the changes you recommended."

Jon and Lance shook hands. Lance departed the building deep in thought. The driver picked Lance up from of the building.

"Mr. Howard, where would you like me to take you?"

"Are there any good places to eat lunch? I want something good like a sandwich but I don't want fast food."

"Mr. Howard, there is a sandwich place down by the medical district near Mercy Hospital that has some good sandwiches, and the ingredients are fresh. It's also a nice place to sit and enjoy the weather, and the scenery if you know what I mean", the driver laughed.

"Yes, drop me off there. I can always take a cab back to the hotel."

"Here you go Mr. Howard. The shop is right in that plaza."

"Thanks. What is your name?"

"John!"

"It's nice to meet you John. I'm Lance Howard, but I'm sure you already knew", Lance laughed. "I will give you a call later if I need you. Thanks again."

Lance walked into the sandwich shop toward the end of the lunch crowd. There were about four people in front of him including an attractive woman in a business suite with a white medical coat. She had olive colored skin with long brown hair. She was talking to one of her colleagues. As her colleague moved up to place her order, Lance seized the opportunity to strike up a conversation.

"This place seems to be very popular. Are they using some special pixie dust to make customers come back?"

The woman laughed as she turned slightly to the side to see the man that made this comment.

"No they don't put pixie dust on the sandwiches. The food here is very good. The ingredients are organic and fresh."

"That is what someone told me. This should be interesting. This is my first time."

"I'm Lance Howard and you are?"

"I'm Julie, Julie Barber."

"Pleased to meet you, Julie. I don't even have to ask. I know you come here often", as he smiled.

"No, it's not like that at all. I usually eat at work,

but I wanted to get out and clear my head because I had some time."

"Oh, where do you work if I'm not being too forward?"

"I work at Mercy Hospital. I'm the hospital administrator there. What about you?" She asked curiously.

"I'm from out of town, but I work in software development. You know anything about software development?"

"I know a little; enough to be dangerous. I can turn my computer on and off, and I use apps on my smart phone. Does that count? " as she smiled, while making eye contact and placing her order.

"What sandwich do you recommend? Remember, it's my first time." Lance grinned.

"The pastrami on wheat is always good."

"I will have the pastrami on wheat with lettuce, tomatoes, and Italian seasoning. Does oregano come in the seasoning?"

"Yes sir."

As Julie and Lance reached the end of the checkout line, Lance gestured to the cashier.

"Combine these two orders."

"No, I can pay for my own lunch." Julie sharply replied.

"No, I insist. It's the least I can do for a lovely lady that gave me a good sandwich recommendation", as he smiled. Julie conceded. As the two walked toward the door and out of the shop, Lance made his latest pitch.

"I know you are at work. However, I would like to take you to lunch tomorrow or at least have one drink with me this evening. It's no obligation, but I would like to have a quiet conversation with you. What do you think?"

"Well lunch probably won't work because my schedule

is packed during the day. I will have one drink with you this evening. Just one drink!"

"Fair enough," as he raised his open hand and cocked his head to the side. "Let's trade business cards. I will write my personal cell number on the back. By the way, where is a good place to have a drink" as he laughed. I was just kidding."

"What works best 7 or 8pm this evening?"

"Seven-thirty is a good time, but I will text or give you a call if things change."

"I will text you the address. I will talk to you later."

Lance took a seat at one of the outside tables as Julie returned to work. Julie smiled as she walked vigorously back to work. Lance admired her curves, as she got further away.

[Phone Rang]

"Hello, this is Lance. Hi Candice, how are things going?"

"I'm doing well. How did your meeting go with your investor and his business partner?

"It wasn't bad. My first investor is still onboard and his business partner is not investing, but he is working to put me in touch with other prospects that may be interested. My investor's business partner invited me to Chicago to discuss some additional details. Overall, it's going well. What's up with you?"

"Wow. That sounds good. Looks like things are coming along well for you. As for me, I have a later flight into Chicago and then a commercial flight to Brazil. I usually don't do commercial flights, but a friend of mine hooked me up. I had a couple of days so I decided to head down that way."

"Oh, interesting. It's a small world. You sure you aren't tracking and stalking me", Lance laughed.

"No, I am not stalking you. If I were, I wouldn't tell you."

"You have a valid point. What time are you getting into Chicago?"

"I should touchdown after 10pm local time. I am so excited about my trip to Brazil even if it's only for a couple of days. I can't wait to stick my toes in the white sandy beach."

"I can only imagine. I know you will be getting in late. Would you like to have a drink later this evening or will it be too late?"

"That would be nice. I know you had to cut our date short last time because of business. I do understand. Maybe you won't get any late night calls from your business partner." She laughed.

"I apologize again. I didn't expect the interruption, but you know business. I may even buy you a drink."

"What! You are kidding. You should buy me several drinks. Wait, I didn't mean it like that", as she laughed.

"You said it. I bet you meant it. Do I have to take you to your meetings on Thursdays?"

"Very funny, I see you got jokes."

"I always had jokes. Why did you think I was stuffy?"

"No, I just didn't think you would be so down to earth. Most people with a lot of money are usually stuffy, uptight, rude, and insulting."

"I understand. I'm not like that at all. My folks taught me better. I can talk rough and insulting to you if you are having withdrawals", he smirked.

"Call me or text me when you land, and we can take it from there."

"I will. Chat with you soon."

* * *

Lance texted Julie the address to the bar. The bar was only a couple of blocks from his hotel. She confirmed and said she would meet him around seven-thirty. Lance spent the remainder of the afternoon on the phone with his staff making the changes Jonathan recommended. Lance was skimming over the local paper when an article caught his eye.

[Local Entrepreneur Is Revolutionizing Hospital Billing]

Lance read the article about Pearson Caldwell. The article mentioned how Caldwell's company continues to make epic strides in changing how hospitals do business. The article mentioned Jonathan Westin as the architect behind Caldwell's successful IPO. I guess Jon is not a bad guy even though he is arrogant and narcissistic.

Lance showered and dressed for his meeting with Julie. He wanted to make a good impression although she has already seen him. Looking through his closet, he chose a dark blue blazer, champagne colored shirt, and dark blue slacks. Lance selected a sleek timepiece to match his attire. Checking the mirror one last time, he headed downstairs and down the street to *Lynx*.

Julie left the office a little earlier than normal. She wanted to impress Lance even though she told herself that this was only a drink, not a date. She rifled through her closet trying to find the perfect outfit for the occasion. She picked a black and beige jump suit to compliment her womanly curves. Julie also decided to wear her hair down, light makeup and pumps to match.

Lance arrived at the bar a little early to get a good seat,

so he could see Julie when she arrived. The bar decor was contemporary, sleek and clean. There were several people already enjoying the transition from their work to an early evening of "happy hour".

Julie walked through the door, looked to her left, and then scanned the rest of the room until she located Lance. Lance helped by raising his hand.

"Hello Julie, it's nice to see you again. Looks like I just saw you not long ago." Lance grinned.

Julie smiled, "I see you moonlight as a comedian".

"I have been known to come up with a joke or two. I'm glad you made it. I wasn't sure you would come."

"I thought about it and decided to live on the edge. Besides, we are meeting in a public place, so I didn't see anything wrong with meeting for a drink."

"Well I'm better now after my therapy. I haven't stalked anyone lately, and I don't listen to those voices in my head." Lance replied with a straight face.

"Well, it was nice meeting you. I will be leaving now. You have issues, and I don't need that kind of drama," Julie said as she gathered her purse to leave.

"I'm only teasing you. I apologize. I didn't mean to scare you or make you feel uncomfortable. Sometimes I play too much. Please accept my apology."

"I will if you promise not to joke about that sort of thing. I have had a bad experience that I care not to talk about, but let's just say it was not a comfortable situation."

"I promise. So what would you like to drink?"

"I would like a margarita with Petron please."

"Hmm, I like a woman that knows what she likes when it comes to the spirits. Waiter, I will have a martini well shaken.

"So have you ever been to this bar?"

"No, I have seen the sign, but I haven't been here. My girlfriends have met at the bar across the street for 'happy hour' a few times, but not here. How did you find this place?"

"I got the recommendations from my driver and the hotel staff."

"You have a driver?"

"Yes, I hired a driver while I'm in town. It's easier to have a driver than taking a taxi. I don't have to worry about being taken somewhere I don't want to go. Besides, I prefer getting to know a person while I'm in town and hiring drivers have really worked for me. Enough about me, tell me about you?"

"What would you like to know", as Julie flashed those hazel eyes at Lance.

"I want to know all your secrets", as he toasted to a new acquaintance.

"I can't tell you those secrets, I may have to kill you", as she laughed.

"I see you have jokes as well. Now, I am afraid."

"That is correct; you should be afraid, be very afraid", as she quenched her lips together and wrinkled her nose.

"Oh my!"

"I'm just teasing you. Seriously, as I told you before, I am a hospital administration, and I have been in the health field for about fifteen years. I am divorced with one son. I lead a pretty simple life doing the normal things as a single parent."

"Interesting. How old is your son?"

"He is twelve. He will be thirteen soon. Now it's your turn."

"Well, I'm single, no kids, and a software developer businessman. I was in college but I didn't finished because

I got bored and wanted to work on my application. I did finish developing the app, and I have enjoyed some professional success."

"That is interesting as well. So it looks like you know what you want to be when you grow up?"

"I guess. I have been in software development for almost ten years now. I'm confident that I know what I am doing, but I am interested in other business ventures. "

"What would you like to do?"

"Although I haven't worked in the field, I'm interested in real estate development. I like the sports management segment of the business. I am currently working on a project for a soccer team in the DC area. Enough about my boring work, and me tell me about hospital administration. What is that like?"

"Your work isn't boring. I am actually interested in finding out about the software side of the business although I don't profess to be an expert. As an administrator, I'm always interested in software that may help my hospital improve operations.'"

The two of them enjoyed their drinks as they got to know each other. Both were intrigued with each other as they established "small talk".

[Phone Rang]

"Hello, this is Lance. Hey Jon, how are things going?

Pause: "Yes, I can meet at 11am. I will see you tomorrow. Thank you."

I apologize for that call. I'm in town to meet with prospective investors on an aforementioned project, and I was confirming a meeting for tomorrow," Lance replied apologetically.

"It's ok. I do understand. I get calls after normal work hours myself. I also used to date a guy that traveled a lot and would often get calls after normal work hours."

"Did he work in IT as well?"

"Yes, he was a software developer in the medical field, so I know a little about the demands of the job", as Julie made eye contact with Lance.

"Having a drink with you has been great, so when can I take you out on a date?"

"You are a busy man from what I can tell", as Julie twirled her hair.

"Well, I can make time", Lance grinned. "I am leaving tomorrow, but I can always come back for a weekend. Have you ever been to San Jose?"

"No, I have been to Los Angeles for a conference, but I haven't been that way in a few years."

"You should consider visiting San Jose. It's green and beautiful", as Lance raised his glass to toast.

"I enjoyed your company, but it's a school night", she smiled.

"I do understand. I can walk you to your car. I wouldn't want anything to happen to you."

"Thank you."

* * *

Lance returned to his hotel and began checking his voice messages and emails. From meeting with Jon to meeting with Julie Barber, his day's agenda had been busy but productive. There was a message from Jon saying he had scheduled Lance to meet with Lucas Cordosa, a Brazilian soccer franchise owner, tomorrow. Good things were on the horizon.

Having a meeting with Lucas Cordosa was critical to building additional investors to the consortium. Brazil was rich in soccer support and to have Lucas onboard would be huge to opening up opportunities not only here domestically but down in Brazil. Lance continued to review his information in preparation of tomorrow's meeting.

[Phone ring]

"Hello, its Lance."

"Hey Lance, this is Candice. I just touched down in Chicago. What are you up to this evening?"

"I'm just going over some prep notes for my upcoming meeting tomorrow. How was your flight? What time does your flight leave tomorrow?"

"My flight was good. I don't leave until 2:20PM, so I can sleep in. It's been a busy week, but I'm looking forward to the getaway."

"Sounds like fun. Have you eaten yet?"

"No, just snacks on the plane. You know they don't feed you on commercial flights", she laughed.

"I do understand. Would you like to grab something to eat? There is a restaurant not far from where I'm staying."

"That sounds good. Let me take a quick shower. What is the address of the restaurant?"

"I'm not really sure. I would have to look it up. How about I send my driver to pick you up? That way you don't have to worry about catching a cab."

"That works for me. I'm at the Brighton at the Chicago O'Hara Airport."

"I will send him out there now. He should be there in about an hour."

The driver arrived at approximately 11pm and waited

for Candice to come down. Lance had already told her what type of car to expect. Minutes later, Candice came down and they were on their way back to Lance's area. Because it was late, traffic was light, which shortened the travel time.

Lance came downstairs and joined Candice on the ride to the restaurant. They both could have walked since it was only a few blocks away, but they decided to ride because it was late.

"It's nice to see you again. This is a pleasant surprise. I didn't expect to see you in Chicago. You sure you aren't following me?"

"I see you have jokes as usual. I don't stalk. Well, I don't admit to stalking", as they both laughed.

The two of them enjoyed a light late night dinner. Lance had already eaten earlier but still had a salad and an appetizer. They walked along the canal enjoying the mild breezy evening. Lance took off his jacket and placed around Candice's shoulders. The two enjoyed laughter and small talk before they returned to the car.

"It's late. You can stay over, and I can have my driver take you back in the morning if you like. I have two queen beds in my suite."

"That would be nice. I am somewhat tired from all of the traveling. I still haven't gotten used to the flying after all these years", as she looked into Lance's eyes and then gazed out into the darkness. Candice found herself wondering what Lance was doing to her. I am having dinner at midnight, and now I'm heading to this man's hotel room. From the plane to his hotel room, all these things are happening way to fast. I definitely need to get a grip on the situation.

"I surmised as much. I know when I fly it takes a lot out of me as well. Would you like some wine?"

"Yes, just one glass. I wouldn't want to get drunk and you take advantage of me."

"Would I do that?" as Lance looked with a devilish grin on his face.

"Sure, tell me anything."

"A toast: To the mile high club!"

"You are wrong for that one", as Candice hit Lance across the arm after the toast. "Why would you make fun of me? You know how embarrassing that was to be doing that on a plane when I was supposed to be working", as she shook her head and eyes rolled.

"But you liked it. It looks like you liked it a lot, given the fact you are in my hotel room."

"I don't know what you are talking about. I'm a good girl."

"Oh really," as Lance pulled her close to give her a romantic kiss. A soft kiss was followed by another one and then a warm embrace. Lance and Candice tongues touched as their kisses became more passionate and intense. Lance hands were rubbing all over her curvaceous hips, up and down her back. Candice breathing got shorter and deeper as Lance kissed her neck. He licked her neck as he turned her around to put his strong arms around her. Candice leaned her head back as she rubbed her hands over Lance's face. He sucked on her earlobes as he breathed on her neck. Lance rubbed her luscious breasts as he began unbuttoning her blouse. Candice nipples were hard as she moaned with excitement. She quickly helped him unbutton her bra to expose her unusually long, aroused nipples.

Lance turned her around as he laid her on the bed, swirling his tongue around her juice soft nipples. Candice pushed Lance's face deep into her breasts. He sucked each tip one by one teasing the tips with his tongue. She arched her back as the intensity increased.

"Lance, you are driving me crazy", as she grabbed a handful of hair.

"I want to please you. Lay back and enjoy the ride. It's time for me to serve you."

Lance swirled his tongue around her belly button. Candice breath got shorter as Lance discovered so many of her sensitive but erotic treasures. He unbuttoned her pants as she laid tensely on the bed. With each button, he licked the opening. Soon, all three buttons were opened and Lance slid her pants off. Candice had on red lace nicely fitted panties to match her lace bra. Lance licked the inside of her leg up one thigh and down the other. He licked the edge of her panties and covered her soft mound with his warm mouth.

"Do you want me to stop?"

"Never, your tongue feels so soft against me body. I feel the heat baby."

Lance pressed his tongue against her soft, newly shaved mound as he grabbed her thighs and then her nipples. Candice moaned with excitement and anticipation. Lance could now feel her wetness. He pulled her panties to the side and lightly licked over her wetness tracing the edges of her sweetness.

"I'm so wet now. Please taste it!"

"Yes, you are wet, "as his tongue went deep inside as his fingers explored her pulsating cave. Lance fingers went in and out until Candice was slippery wet.

"Give it to me baby," she said. "I want it now."

Lance slid inside of her with ease and filled her with his engorged cock. Candice exhaled and grabbed his back pulling him deeper inside. He went deep inside and then pulled out. He teased her with the tip of his manhood; rubbing it up and down on her clit until she almost exploded.

"Get on my back baby. I want to feel you deep inside of me", as she rolled over on her stomach. Lance stretched her arms out over her head as he entered her from the back. Candice arched her hips for easy entry.

"Oh baby!" She uttered in a husky voice. Lance hips moved round and round as he went deep inside. Slow, deep strokes followed by sudden hard strokes drove Candice over the edge. She vigorously pushed her hips into Lance as the intensity continued. Lance put his hand on her shoulder with the other one grabbing a handful of her ebony hair. He pumped her hard and fast for a few minutes before Candice exploded with ecstasy. Moments later, Lance core coiled until he exploded inside filling her with his hot juices. They both were covered with sweat as they crossed the edge of release and relaxation.

[Phone Rang]

"Mr. Howard, this is Ms. Salazar's personal assistant. I sent you an email confirming your appointment with Ms. Salazar on the 20th of next month. If you have any questions or need to reschedule, let me know."

"Thanks for the call. I will accept the invitation."

Lance rolled over to see Candice still sleeping. She was snoring lightly but not annoying. With the busy week, travel, and late night extracurricular activities, Candice took advantage of the restful moment. Lance got up and did his normal workout before hitting the shower. He wanted to go over the presentation notes a couple more times before his meeting with Jon and Lucas. Lance's focus was to get a face-to-face meeting with Lucas. Jon had set the introduction up so he couldn't blow this opportunity. Lucas was an extremely busy and powerful man. If Lance could get Lucas on board, he may "pave the way" for other power players.

Lance ordered room service for Candice and himself. Soon, there was a knock on the door causing Candice to turn over still appearing loopy.

"Good morning sleeping beauty. I see you are finally awake", Lance grinned.

"Good morning. How are you? What time is it?" as she hugged the pillow.

"It's a little after 9am. What time do you have to be there?"

"Not anytime soon, I was just checking."

"I have a meeting at 11am, but you are welcome to stay and relax. It shouldn't take that long. I can have my driver drop you at the airport, if that works."

"That would be great. I would really appreciate that a lot."

"I will be leaving in the next 30 minutes, so I can get to the office and go over my notes."

"Yes, I need to get up and take a shower. What did you order for breakfast?"

"I ordered the usual breakfast stuff, fruit, eggs, toast, coffee, etc."

"I could get used to this treatment. You know how to spoil a girl", as Candice went to wash her face.

The two of them ate breakfast and talked on the balcony.

It was a clear day. Both enjoyed each other's company as time began to slip away.

"I would love to enjoy this beautiful morning, but I have to get going. Perhaps we can pick this fun time up after my meeting?"

"I would like that a lot before I have to head to the airport."

Lance gave Candice a big hug and a light kiss on the lips. It was already close to 10am, and he didn't want to be late.

"I will call you when my meeting is over."

"Sounds good", as Candice watched Lance walk out of the hotel room. Her mind wondered as her thoughts took her back to last night's escapades. Her time with Lance was always intense and satisfying. She thought to herself, Lance is an awesome lover. He always takes me places and I always enjoy the ride. Candice also hoped Lance's meeting didn't take too long so she could spend more time with him before heading to Brazil.

* * *

Lance met Jon at his office around ten-forty five. The two men exchanged pleasantries.

"Lance, I'm glad you could make it. I know it was short notice. I have arranged a video conference call with Lucas Cardoso. During the call, I can introduce you to him, and you can take it from there. I wouldn't try to pitch him over the video but get to know him a little better. I don't know if you are familiar with the business customs in South America, but people there spend a lot of time getting to know a person before they discuss business. It's almost time for the call. I will have one of my assistance come in and get things ready."

"Thanks for the information."

"Good morning Lucas, how are you today? How is the weather there?"

"Good morning Jon. It's been a long time since we last spoke. How have you been? I am doing well. The weather here is warm and nice as usual. I don't see how you stand that cold, winter weather there."

"I have gotten used to the snow, but I know I can visit warm places in winter when the cold gets to be more than I can bear. Do I still have an open invitation down there?"

"Sure, just let me know. You can always visit. I don't have to be here."

"How is the family?"

"All is well. Elena is doing well, keeping busy by spending my money. My son just finished law school, so another shark has been released into the wild", as he chuckled. "My daughter just started graduate school for business. Perhaps she will take over the family business. Who knows? Yes, things are going well. What about you? Have you found that special lady yet?"

"No, I haven't found that special one yet."

"You have to stop working so much and enjoy life."

"I know; I will slow down soon."

"You mentioned you have an acquaintance you wanted to introduce me to for a possible business venture."

"Yes, he is sitting to my right. Lance Howard, this is Lucas Cardoso. Lucas is a major player in the cell phone industry in South America and a soccer enthusiast."

"You always give me exceptional introductions. Please to meet you Lance. Tell me about yourself. What do you do for work; outside interests, etc.?"

"Please to meet you too, Mr. Cardoso."

"Call me Lucas."

"Lucas, I'm a software developer of an application that compresses video and allows users to share on their mobile devices. This app provides users an efficient management tool for their data and memory on their devices. As for outside interests, I enjoy reading, water sports, and chess."

"That is an interesting blend of activities. You married?"

"No, I'm single."

"Good for you. Take your time and find the right one."

"So what is this business venture?"

"I'm working toward establishing a soccer franchise to include a stadium in the Washington DC area. I would be happy to come down and discuss the details in person."

"Yes, I would like to hear the details, so set something up with me later this month." Lance took notes and mentioned he would coordinate with Jon for Lucas's personal assistant to get on Lucas's calendar. Jon's meeting soon wrapped up and was a success. Jon filled Lance in on the details and background on Lucas. The two men have known each other for years and had done some business ventures together. Although they didn't talk often, they still maintained a solid business relationship.

"So that went well I believe. I did what you advised about not trying to pitch my idea. Lucas seems affable, with an even-keeled disposition."

"I see you did follow my advice. Don't let Lucas's easygoing personality deceive you. He is a hard nose businessman and wouldn't be worth billions with an "s" if he didn't know how to get things done. Although he does has a passion for soccer, he is a businessman first and foremost."

"I will definitely take your advice into consideration. Well I am going to get going so I can head back to California. I have lots of work to catch up on. Thank you again for your time and the introduction."

"You are welcome. I'm glad I can help", as Jon shook his hand, grinned, and nodded. Lance left the office heading back to his hotel room. His driver was waiting outside.

Moments later, Jon called Lucas back to discuss the meeting.

"Jon, is everything going according to plan?"

"Yes, everything is on-track. I told him that you were a nice guy but a tough business man and that he would have to come down to visit in person to convince you to invest," as Jon sighed with a devilish gesture.

"I can't believe he fell for that routine. He is more naive than we expected. I will continue to play along and keep things interesting. Do you believe he can pull this venture off?"

"I'm not sure but he has a lot of heart so we will see. The worst case scenario, we will benefit from the outcome either way."

"I will keep you posted on how things progress when he comes down to visit. I love these deals. We have been doing these things for how many years now?"

"I'm guessing maybe 10 years now", as both men chuckled.

Lance was heading back to the hotel when he got a phone call.

"Hey Julie, how are you today?

"I'm doing well. Did I catch you at a bad time?"

"No, I'm good. I just got out of a meeting. What's going on in your world?"

"I wanted to give you a quick call. I had a mini break in my day and wanted to give you a shout. Have you concluded all your business in Chicago?"

"Yes, for now but I'm working a new business relationship in the area. That means I will be traveling this way on a regular basis. Why do you ask?"

"I was only wondering. I enjoyed our drink and conversation."

"So did I. How about I take you to dinner when I'm in town next time?"

"That sounds good. Just let me know."

"I will give you a call and let you know when I will be in town, that way, you can pencil me into your busy schedule", as he grinned.

"It's not like that at all", as she twirled the hair between her fingers.

"I see. I was only teasing you. That sounds good. I will chat with you soon."

Lance continued to review several work related emails about his software company. Although the company had a CEO, Lance kept a close "eye" on his company's operations. Traffic was a little heavy, so he took advantage of the time.

Candice texted him: give me a call when you get out of your meeting. Lance called Candice to let her know he was on his way.

"Candice, are you still at the hotel?"

"Yes, I fell back asleep. I took a shower, had some breakfast, and drifted off. I'm sorry I was being lazy."

"It's ok to be lazy. I know you work hard."

"How did your meeting go?"

"It went well. I was introduced to a prospective investor,

but I have to follow up to continue to foster the relationship. The prospect lives in Brazil but I'm not sure exactly where. I still have some work to do. I will have my admin coordinate and get me the specifics. We can talk more when I get back there."

"I will see you when you get back."

Lance arrived back at the hotel approximately 15 minutes later. Lance went up through the lobby to the elevator. He quickly reached his floor and opened the door.

"Candice, are you decent", he voiced in a concerning tone.

"Yes, I'm decent. I have on a robe and underwear. It's not like you haven't seen the goods" she replied in a sarcastic voice. Lance grinned as he looked at her. Her eyes told him she wanted him and missed his touch the short amount of time he was away at his meeting.

"Aww, did you miss me?"

"No!" as she turned her back with her, arms folded.

"You did", as he turned her around and pulled her close to him. Lance held her face in his strong hands as he gave her passionate kisses, licking up her lips. Their tongues touched and the intensity grew. He grabbed Candice as she wrapped her legs around him as he ran his fingers through her hair.

Deep kisses continued until Candice's robe fell to the floor. Lance loosened his tie, unbuttoned his shirt as he continued the intense kisses. Soon, Lance swirled Candice around and bent her over the kitchen table. He ran his fingers through her hair with his other hand on her shoulder. Lance licked the back of her neck. Candice let out a loud moan of pure pleasure. He quickly unbuttoned his pants and kicked off his shoes.

Candice looked back at him and gave him a passionate, wet kiss as her breathing got shorter. Lance continued to press his brawny masculine body against her curvaceous hips and thighs. She could feel his hardness through his underwear. Her pond of passion was pulsating and throbbing at this point. His strong hands gently squeezed the inside of her thighs making their way up to the edge of her treasure. Her love cave began to throb even more in anticipation as her erotic juices began to overflow and run down her leg.

"Why are you toying with me? I'm so wet right now."

"I like it's wet, creamy and steamy. When I put it inside I want you to explode and I don't think you are ready to explode yet."

"Don't make me beg," Candice replied in a huskily voice. "I've been on fire since this morning."

Lance put his finger inside of her and then sucked his finger to taste her natural juices. In an instance, he turned Candice around, lifted her, and sat her on the counter. He fell to his knees, aggressively pulled her to the edge of the counter with his strong arms, draping her legs over his shoulders. His soft warm tongue licked the inside of her thighs, up one thigh and then down the other. Candice moaned with excitement as she grabbed two handfuls of Lance's hair pulling his head into her treasure. Lance's tongue lightly glided over the contours of her womanly lips.

Candice uttered a loud moan as her juices squirted and ran down her thighs. Lance tongue continued tracing her womanly lips, curling his tongue upward on her hot pink button of excitement.

"You going to make me cum if you continue doing that," she whispered.

"That was my plan all along anyway. You need the release; you need to be taken care of in all the right ways." Lance rose from his knees, bent Candice over the counter, and slid inside of her wetness. He continued to go in and out as she arched her back and grinded her hips against him. With his hands on her shoulders while grabbing a hand full of hair, Lance body grew in intensity the faster he pumped. Soon, his body exploded releasing his load deep inside of her. Her body tensed with excitement and release as she cascaded over the climatic waterfall.

Candice and Lance both breathed heavily for several minutes as the orgasmic excitement eventually returned them to a normal state. They both lay on the sofa relishing in the moment.

"I hate to get up. I have to catch a plane in 90 minutes. At least, I don't have to check any luggage and security should be a breeze."

"Yes, I need to get going myself. I have a charter at 3:30pm so I think I will get an early start. We can ride out to the airport together."

"That sounds good. I had a great time as always."

"So did I."

Chapter 4

M ONICA Salazar is a real estate veteran in the Washington DC area. She has been in the business for almost 20 years. She started as a leasing agent when she was in college to help pay for school. Although she wasn't an agent, she learned a lot about the business through her constant interaction with clients, tenants, and agents. After graduating with her degree in business administration, she got a job as an administrative assistant in one of the largest real estate brokerages in the DC area. Monica was assertive early in her real estate career. She spent extra time learning every aspect of her job and all other jobs in the brokerage firm. Monica seized every opportunity to learn something new.

There was an opening for a lead administrator in Philadelphia. Monica was young, adventurous, and single, so she didn't hesitate. She packed her things and moved to Philly. Things were going well at first. It was a new job, new city, and new surroundings. As an artsy outgoing person, she was able to make friends and enjoy the many cultural events Philadelphia had to offer.

Things at work were going well. Monica had a lot of responsibility early with her new job. She oversaw all administrative paperwork and a staff of fifteen junior admin assistants. The Philly office supported five other offices in the greater Philadelphia area. Monica worked in the central headquarters office that supported 50 agents. This was a lot of responsibility for a 25-year-old recent graduate. However, Monica had worked in the real estate business for three years prior to her graduation.

Most of her colleagues were friendly and cooperative with the exception of a few. Barbara Sanford was the distinctive exception. Unknowingly, Monica accepted the lead administrator role. She didn't know that management had demoted the previous person in the position to create the opening for Monica. Barbara Sanford was a middle-aged administrative manager that had worked for the brokerage firm for twenty-two years. She was close to an early retirement. Over the last three years, Barbara's work performance suffered. She was constantly making minor mistakes not expected for a seasoned manager. Real estate paperwork was often lost and had to be redone creating embarrassing moments with a few of the agents. After going through a nasty divorce, Barbara started drinking more. Her two adult children were constantly having financial difficulties; expecting their mother to help them work through their challenges. Because of her long-standing relationship with the brokerage owners, the managing partner decided to demote her instead of firing her outright. She held some responsibilities but these were limited to a specific group of low valued accounts. Barbara only needed three more years to retire so it was just a matter of time. Francis Holland, the managing broker, picked up most of the slack and spread the work across several of the more experienced admin assistants.

Tension continued between Barbara and Monica. Barbara couldn't deal with the fact that she had been demoted because of a young unknown from out of town.

[I can't believe Francis would promote her over me. I have been with this brokerage firm for over 22 years. I guess that is how things work when you get older. Management just puts people out and replaces them with new inexperience people. I don't understand how management could so casually minimize my value. I was with this firm when they were struggling during the recession of the 1990s. I just don't understand.]

Monica's career continued to soar as she took on more responsibility. After five years in the business, Monica finally earned her brokerage license. She was so excited that she wanted to share with everyone. There was a congratulatory party coming up in June to celebrate all new licensees and brokers. Barbara saw this event as the perfect opportunity to "rain on Monica's parade".

The event was a huge success. Everyone enjoyed and congratulated the newly minted agents and brokers. There was one celebratory toast after another.

"Hello Monica." Barbara spoke in a trite tone.

"Hello Barbara!"

"Monica, I see you finally got your broker's license. It's about time," Barbara replied in a divisive and sharp tone.

"I'm surprise it took so long. I know you've had Francis "around your finger" for the last couple of years. You have so many people fooled but not me. I can see right through your games and your so-called charm. I think you are just a pretty face that slept her way to the top."

"Wow! I see someone has some bitterness. I will share

some things with you. First, I do my job well, and I'm effective (something you wouldn't know about); secondly, I don't have codependent children that expect their parents to "bail them out" every time they hit a "bump" in the road of life; and lastly, have you been going to your AA meeting like you were supposed to go. I will attend with you if my presence will help. I know how important moral support is when you are dealing with alcoholism. Just let me know and I will make myself available." Monica calmly replied as she turned to walk away and continued mingling.

Barbara was outraged and frustrated. All the things Monica said were true. She hated the fact that Monica was right. Barbara had all those problems and issues in her life. She failed once again to show how Monica was ineffective as a professional and as a person. Her sinister plan had failed.

Monica's career was on the fast track as she continued up the corporate ladder. Eventually, Monica was managing high value residential properties and aggressively moving into the commercial segment of the business. As her business acumen increased, she was able to effective compete in a highly segmented and male dominated commercial real estate environment. Eventually, her career aspirations reached a plateau. With 'office politics' being a possible factor, Monica was passed over as the next managing broker of the commercial segment. Because of the promotion pass over, Monica left and started her own brokerage firm.

Monica's brokerage firm struggled for the first six months of operations. Running a brokerage firm was not as easy as she thought. Although Monica worked night and day to build the infrastructure of her business, her health and sales suffered as a result. Things were not going well with the economy. Monica opened her brokerage firm 18 months before the 'meltdown' in the housing industry in 2008. Her projections, along with many industry projections, were wrong and under estimated the dismal outcome.

To add insult to injury, Monica personal life was a disaster as well. Her marriage was falling apart. Her husband, Frank, wanted a family. The couple had discussed having children later when Monica's career was at a stable place. With her departure from the previous employer's brokerage firm and the launch of her own endeavor, now wasn't a good time to start a family. With this being a deciding factor, Frank filed for divorce within six months after Monica launched her brokerage firm. Frank didn't contest for joint ownership in the budding company. They both amicably dissolved their marriage. Monica was devastated over the divorce. She didn't expect her marriage to end at a point when she needed her husband's support as she faced the challenges of starting a new company. Between building the business and the end of her marriage, Monica was emotionally "empty". She doubted her confidence, questioned her sanity, and spiraled to her lowest point mentally.

Having struggled most of her life, Monica continued building her business one client at a time. A few of her loyal clients came onboard with her new venture. After a few years, the economy recovered and the real estate business began its comeback. Monica was able to hire more agents as her business quickly expanded along the East Coast. Monica continued to nurture her network of powerful contacts within the real estate industry through joint ventures, mergers and a few acquisitions. She bought a couple of boutique real estate agencies in niche markets. She continued to foster her political connections as well. In the DC area, nothing happens without the right connection. In a highly political environment, it's not whom you know but who knows you. Monica worked hard to build her small empire and her success eventually flourished.

[Five Years Earlier]

Monica had recently finalized her divorce from Frank. She could not believe she was divorced from the man she thought she would spend the rest of her life. Frank was a gynecologist and enjoyed his work. However, Frank came from a large family with four brothers. He always wanted a moderate size family of three children and a dog. Although he had the dog, he longed for children. He always wanted a daughter because there were no girls when he was growing up. Many of his patients would bring their daughters to their appointments. He often took that opportunity to interact with the children by giving them candy, with their parent's permission of course.

Some of his patients admired his patience with children. They saw that as an attractive characteristic of a parent. Those same patients often asked him if he had children. Disappointedly, he told them no. On one occasion, a patient's friend saw the doctor as a viable "catch" as her friend was making her next appointment. Frank was a tall attractive man with dark hair and piercing blue eyes. His voice was deep and authoritative with a sense of calmness.

"Francine, I will see you back in a few months for your follow-up appointment. Let me know if you have any issues with your new medicines."

"Francine, aren't you going to introduce me?"

"Dr. Salazar, I would like to introduce you to my friend

Danielle", as she awkwardly looked at her, frowning and rolling her eyes.

"It's a pleasure to meet you Dr. Salazar. Francine tells me you have been her doctor for years now. I guess you are a great doctor. I'm sure your hands are gentle, and she feels comfortable with you", as she looked into those blue eyes, shook his hand and paused for a moment. As Frank realized what was taking place, he smiled, and nodded.

"It is a pleasure to meet you. However, I have a busy schedule today. Perhaps we can speak the next time", as he politely excused himself. Frank was a married man. Although women often propositioned him, he maintained his loyalty to Monica. Monica, on the other hand, was married to her profession. She intensely focused on advancing her career. In the highly competitive world of real estate, if a person weren't assertive, that person would often see opportunities pass them by. As a woman and a minority, Monica felt she had to be twice as good as her male counterparts to be effective and compete in the male dominating sector of commercial real estate.

Frank and Monica grew in different directions and ultimately grew apart. The couple eventually began living separate lives within the same house. Monica continued to focus her efforts toward fostering her career. She took additional classes, went to professional seminars, and attended several conferences. Because Frank was well established in his career, Frank's focus was toward settling down and having children. Frank, seven years Monica's senior, felt it was the right time to start a family.

The couple went on what turned out to be their last vacation. As they were enjoying Paris for two weeks, Frank saw this trip as the perfect time to have the conversation again about starting a family.

"Frank, it's so nice here in France."

"I know, the architecture is amazing. There is so much to see and do. We have been to the Eiffel tower, the Louvre Museum, and a host of other museums. I'm glad you talked me into taking this vacation. I know I have been working too much lately. I realized I was becoming a workaholic, but you know I really enjoy what I do."

"I know sweetheart. However, we do have to live a little and enjoy life", as the couple made their way back to their luxury suite with a balcony overlooking the garden.

"I know. I have to learn to relax."

"Speaking about relaxing, have you thought anymore about us starting a family? I'm not a 'spring chick' and I would at least like to be young enough to enjoy our children growing up. We do well financially, so I think it's a good time to start a family. Besides, don't you want a cute little girl or boy or both?" as he gave her a warm hug.

"I understand. Remember we discussed starting a family once I made managing broker over the commercial segment. Because of the highly male dominated environment, the executives would just use the fact of my family as a discriminating factor. We both know it's not fair, but that is the reality."

"So when do you think you may get promoted?"

"I believe senior management will make a decision in the next couple of months. I have been hearing those rumors. Currently, the selection is between myself and another broker, but I have a couple more years of experience."

"Monica, you have been telling me to hold on for years

now. When we got married, you said you wanted to wait so you could get your broker's license. Now, you have your broker's license. You asked me to wait until you got promoted to managing broker over the commercial segment. If you get that promotion, there will be something else. I really don't think you really want children", as his tone and demeanor changed. Frank, frustrated, left the room and went out on the balcony for some fresh air.

After a few moments, Monica joined him on the balcony.

"Honey, I'm sorry if I upset you. I know you are frustrated. I ask that you only be patience with me just a little while longer; at least over the next few months."

"I will wait and see how the next few months unfold."

Monica didn't get promoted. Management promoted one of Monica's male counterparts over her. Senior management didn't provide her a good explanation, but encouraged her that her time was coming soon and that the organization had something special for her. Deeply discouraged and devastated by the news, Monica took matters into her own hand.

"Monica, I'm sorry you didn't get promoted. I know how much getting promoted meant to you. You have only been at the agency a few years. Perhaps in the next six months, senior management will open up a specific division tailored for you," Frank compassionately replied when he learned his wife didn't get promoted.

"Not the next six months or the next six years, I'm not staying at this agency," she sharply replied. "You sound like the men at the agency. I'm not going to lie down and take this treatment. I am going to do something about this situation," she angrily replied.

"Honey, don't do anything unreasonable. You have

worked so hard to earn your broker's license. Don't do anything that would jeopardize your career."

"I'm not going to do anything that will jeopardize my career. Actually, I'm going to do something that I should have done a long time ago."

"What would that be?"

"I'm going to start my own real estate brokerage. I have been working in the field almost 10 years now. I have reach the plateau at this agency, and I don't want to start all over at another one."

"Do you think you are ready for this level of responsibility?"

"There you go doubting my ability as well. I have enough of that at work. I didn't expect to have this sort of doubt at home. I expected you would be excited not questioning my ability."

"I'm not doubting your ability, I'm just trying to be the voice of reason."

"Is that what you call it?"

"There is no need to lash out at me. I'm on your side."

"Are you really? From what I can see, you are behaving like all the other men in my office; questioning my ability to do a job. Could it be that you doubt me because I am a woman?"

"No, I don't feel that way at all."

"You have your career. You have a well-established practice with a group of doctors. Things are going well for you. Things are not as rosy in my world. I have worked my whole life to build a solid career. Now, I am being told that I do a good job but not good enough to lead and manage a key business unit in the organization."

Frank decided to discontinue the conversation with Monica. She was angry and irrational. He decided to give her some time before readdressing the situation. At this point, Monica was extremely volatile, and he didn't want to escalate a situation unnecessarily. Frank knew now was not a good time to discuss starting a family. Frank knew discussing starting a family now might send Monica over the edge with anger and resentment.

Monica continued her efforts to start her own agency. Monica changed her attitude forever. Her whole focus and passion was to establish her own agency. All her actions pointed toward building the infrastructure to get her budding business off the ground. While at work, she looked for ways to gain a competitive edge by looking at the current agency's processes and determining ways to incorporate those ideas into her own agency. Monica efforts and actions became all consuming. In her mind, nothing really mattered other than starting her own business. As a result, her marriage began to suffer. Frank and Monica spent less and less time together. When they did share time together, real estate and the business dominated the conversations. Almost every discussion about starting a family ended in a nasty argument between the couple. Sometimes, the two of them didn't speak for days.

Frank suggested to Monica that they go to marriage counseling. He wanted to save the marriage. Monica initially agreed but later rejected the idea by canceling the appointments just before the appointment date. Communication between the two became toxic. Monica stopped cooking most of the time and cooking was something she enjoyed. She was an excellent cook; one of the things Frank found so attractive about her. Now, most of Monica's meals were take-out because she didn't want to waste valuable time cooking. She decided that cooking was too domestic for her.

"Monica, what is going on lately? You have all but stopped cooking. Why have you given up cooking?"

"I didn't give up cooking. I stopped cooking because I didn't see cooking as being that important. Besides, cooking is domestic. I have a business to build and run and cooking is not my priority. If you want a meal, you can always order something. We make enough money between the two of us that you can eat out every night and not go broke," she sarcastically responded.

"And another thing, I'm not the only person that can cook. You can cook as well. Just because I used to cook most of the meals doesn't mean you can't get your hands dirty and prepare a meal every once in a while," as she rolled her eyes, turned her back, and continued typing on the computer.

"Monica, what is wrong with you. You are obsessed with starting your company. Is starting your company worth tearing your marriage apart?"

"You don't cook, or clean and we don't talk anymore."

"If you want a cook and a maid, Here is the phone book; it's full of maids and catering services," as she threw the phonebook at Frank.

"I ain't the fucking maid. I'm tired of men thinking I'm only good for their own satisfaction or good for doing domestic chores. Those days are over. I will hire someone to do my domestic activities", as she stormed out of the room and slammed the door.

Monica irrational behavior left Frank dumbfounded. He didn't know what came over her. Frank had to handle the situation with Monica very delicately because of her anger and resentment toward men, the world, and her professional position.

Over the next few months, Monica and Frank marriage continued to deteriorate as the couple grew more and more distance. Soon they were sleeping in separate bedrooms. Because Monica was often up late and grew tired of Frank complaining, she decided to move her office to a bedroom in the basement. The couple was on two different sleep schedules.

The couple used to have a health sex life. Because of Monica grueling schedule, the couple's sex life became almost inexistence. Monica often worked over 17 hours a day, seven days a week. She was literally exhausted when it was time for bed. Frank reached his breaking point after almost five months.

"Monica, we need to talk."

"What would you like to talk about?" as she sat on the sofa.

"I know you are working hard to grow your business. However, over the last six months, you have been neglecting me. I'm your husband, but you haven't been treating me like your husband lately. We don't talk, you stopped taking care of the house, and you stopped cooking. Also, we haven't made love in almost six months. You have been angry and edgy for a long time. Is there something going on", as he spoke with concern and uncertainty.

"There is nothing going on here. I'm working hard to build my business. I have been putting in the time to make my business successful. I'm sorry if I haven't had time to clean the house, cook, and fuck you when you want me to," she sharply responded.

"Do you want to fuck? We can do that right now", as she opened her legs and leaned back on the sofa. "Let's get this over with so I can go back to what I was doing. I'm tired of men thinking that women's only purpose is to satisfy their needs."

"That is not what I meant at all. You misunderstood me."

"Now, I'm too dumb to understand. What will it be next?"

"Monica, I believe you are being unreasonable," he responded in a calm voice of reason.

"I'm being unreasonable now. What will it been next? Perhaps you will say I'm being emotional, and I can't handle the pressure of running a business and having a balanced life", as Monica stormed out of the room.

Frank was at a loss. Monica was bitter toward men, the marriage, and anything that didn't involve fostering her business. Things between them continued to deteriorate to the point where Frank could no longer take this abusive treatment and filed for divorce.

Monica was somewhat surprised, but not really. She thought her husband would be there to support her career endeavors but then she had been bitter toward men and quickly turned resentful toward Frank. She felt Frank was abandoning her and disappointing her like most men in her life. After the initial shock, Monica decided it was best for her and Frank to part ways. With the freedom, she could pursue her business full speed ahead without the guilty and resentment associated with being married and having to choose between him and her career. Monica made a pledge to herself that from this point onward, she would focus on her business and take a break emotionally from relationships for a while.

Weeks turned into months, and soon Monica's divorce was final. Through the hurt and disappointments both personally and professionally, Monica persevered. She was determine to build her business at all costs. Emotionally, Monica did take a break. For the first year after her divorce, she didn't date or even have a sexual relationship with anyone. This was her time to heal and grow.

A few years after the recession and the real estate market meltdown, things began to turn around for Monica. She was adding new clients one by one. Although she had left her previous agency, a few of her loyal clients followed her to her own agency. Her hard work was finally beginning to pay off. She continued to be active in the DC political landscape by attending several gala events. Monica saw these events as excellent networking opportunities to establish her agency's brand and get to know the "power players" in Washington. During one of the gala event, she met Jonathan Westin.

"Monica it's so nice to see you again", as Ashley Patterson extended her hand. Ashley Patterson was a prominent lobbyist on Capitol Hill. As a long-time lobbyist, Ashley had an extensive circle of powerful friends.

"It's good to see you as well."

"Come I want to introduce you to Jonathan Westin. Jonathan Westin is a venture capitalist that does business across the country and around the world", as the two women walked toward him as he was drinking champagne and mingling.

"Monica, I would like to introduce you to Jonathan Westin. Jonathan is a prominent businessman from Chicago. Monica's real estate agency handles and manages key properties in the DC area", as the two exchange pleasantries. Ashley quietly excused herself and continued mingling.

"It's a pleasure to meet you Mr. Westin."

"Call me Jonathan", as his eyes narrowed as the two of them made eye contact. Monica's beauty, her assertiveness, and her curvaceous figure impressed Jonathan. Within a couple of minutes, Monica established rapport and pitched her business to the prominent businessman from Chicago.

"Interesting, I see you know your business and market very well."

"Yes, it's important to provide my clients with boutique professional but personalized service", as Monica presented Jon her card and obtained his card as well. Monica clearly saw Jonathan as a prospective client. However, Jonathan saw Monica from a personal perspective.

CHAPTER 5

THREE months later, Jon called Monica.

"Salazar Realty, how may I direct your call," the receptionist replied in a warm friendly voice.

"I would like to speak to Monica Salazar please", Jon spoke in his deep resonating voice.

"Who shall I say is calling," the receptionist replied.

"Tell her Jonathan Westin from Chicago."

Moments later, "This is Monica."

"Monica, I will be in town on business. I have some commercial properties for one of my businesses. I would like to meet and discuss. I will be in town tomorrow. What is your availability?"

"What time tomorrow are you in town and when would you like to meet?"

"I should arrive early morning but I was looking at meeting early afternoon, around 1-2pm timeframe. Will that timeframe work?"

"That timeframe will be perfect. Give me a call and we can set up a meeting place", as she gave Jon her cell number.

"I will speak with you tomorrow", as Jon ended the call.

"Sara, reschedule my appointments for tomorrow afternoon. I need to be available."

The next day, Monica met Jonathan at a quiet, but prominent restaurant for business luncheons.

"I'm glad you could meet me on such short notice."

"No, it was not a problem at all," Monica politely replied.

"Monica, I have several properties in the DC area. I am looking for a real estate firm that can effectively manage the leasing of commercial space. I haven't had much success in the past with local agencies. Those agencies were more concerned about the residential segment of the market. My experience has been less than favorable with commercial brokerages with most of them taking a hands-off approach. The bottom line, I am looking at an agency that takes care of my properties with minimum involvement on my part. I have several warehouses that house a wine and spirits distribution company. I've had several problems because these properties are older. I'm interested in turning these properties over to your agency if you can give me a level of assurance you can effectively manage them."

"Jonathan, like I told you when we met at the gala, my agency provides personalized but professional services."

"I'm willing to give your agency an opportunity. We will have an exclusive agreement for a six-month trial period. Afterwards, we will agree to a one year contract and review the arrangement annually to evaluate if the business relationship will continue."

"That sounds fair enough," Monica replied.

"I will have my people send the contract to your office."

"Thank you", as Monica shook Jon's hand.

"Now that the business is out of the way, what are you plans for dinner?" as Jon's piercing eyes looked through Monica.

"I have plans," Monica firmly replied although she didn't have any plans for the evening. "Perhaps we can have dinner another time when you are in town again."

"Definitely, I will hold you too it," as Jon cracked a slight smile.

Monica and Jonathan business relationship continued. The initial contractual period ended and Monica's agency agreed to manage several of Jonathan's warehouses. Although Jonathan was unable to establish a personal relationship with Monica, the two enjoyed a profitable and long-standing business relationship.

Monica finally saw the tide turn. Her budding business of only a few short years had grown into a formidable boutique size commercial brokerage firm. She began to enjoy the rewards of her efforts. Monica decided to take a vacation. She hadn't taken a vacation in years. Emotionally, she was ready to begin dating again. First, she was long overdue for a much-needed vacation. Secondly, she was ready to have a meaningful relationship. Monica booked her flight and vacation to Rome, Italy.

Monica enjoyed spending two weeks in Rome. She visited all of the typical tourist attractions but wanted to experience some of the local population and cuisine. As an avid connoisseur of fine wines, she wanted to experience Italy's finest wineries. Monica used her diverse contacts to obtain an invitation to the Li Volsi Vineyard wine tasting event. An invitation to a wine tasting event at the Li Volsi Spirits, LTD, one of the oldest and most prominent family owned wine and spirits companies in Rome was an indicator of elite statue. This wine tasting event was by invitation only. There were about 30 guests attending the event.

Monica didn't actually know any of the guests, but knew how to network effectively. Shortly after arriving, she had introduced herself to a few people and shared in stimulating conversations about wines.

Vito Li Volsi always attended the three annual wine tasting events at his vineyard. He took these opportunities to meet people that actually drank his wines and spirits. Vito seized the opportunity to get direct feedback on the products.

"Hello, my dear; I don't think I've had the pleasure of meeting you," he spoke is a soothing cordial voice with a heavy Italian accent.

"My name is Monica Salazar", as she gracefully extended her hand.

"I am Vito Li Volsi. It is a pleasure to make your acquaintance", as he gently kissed her hand.

Monica blushed, eyes rolled as she showed her beautiful pearly white teeth. Her eyebrows raised as she experienced this charming olive skin man kiss her hand. Although Vito was balding, he was still an attractive man with chiseled cheekbones and caramel colored eyes.

Monica's beauty captivated Vito's attention as well. Monica's long mocha colored hair complimented her brown sugar-colored skin, natural rose-colored lips, and hazel eyes. At 5 feet 10 inches tall, Monica's curvaceous hips, long legs, and voluptuous breasts often drew men's attention often before she said a word.

"It's a pleasure to meet you as well," she politely replied. "I see you enjoy the wines and spirits."

"Yes, I enjoy a fine wine. A woman is like a fine wine as well: Takes time to perfect, very satisfying to the palate, and leaves a lasting impression."

Monica eyes widened, rolled, as she smiled once again. Vito had captured Monica's attention.

"I don't mean to be forward, but take a walk with me", as he gestured the way. Monica followed, as she wanted to learn more about this fascinating man.

"Monica, where are you from and what do you do", Vito inquired.

"I'm from the US and I own a real estate agency. What about you; what do you do?"

"I am in the wines and spirits business. It's a good line of work", as he modestly responded. "What brings you to Italy?"

"Actually, a large plane with other passengers", she wittingly replied.

"I see you are smart, witty, and funny", as he laughed.

"I do my best. Seriously, I am in Italy for vacation or as you say in Europe: holiday."

"I see. So how do you like it so far? Have you been to Italy before?"

"No, this is my first time. I must say, I am enjoying my vacation thus far. The Italian people have been warm and hospitable."

"Yes, we Italians believe in living life."

"Interesting, my Venezuelan heritage shares a similar philosophy. My mother is from Venezuela; my father is American."

The two continued to talk and became better acquainted. The more they talked, the more they realized the things they shared in common. Vito asked Monica to dinner and she accepted. The two shared interesting conversations, delectable wine, and cuisine. After dinner, the couple went for a walk along the pier enjoying the water.

Over the next few days, Vito showed Monica various tourist and historical sites around Rome. Monica enjoyed the companionship, the conversations, and the adventures. Vito was warm, caring, and compassionate. Monica relaxed around Vito, showing her wit, humor, and funny personality.

While dining near Monica's hotel, the couple shared a festive time as the two had done all of the previous evenings. After dinner, Monica invited Vito to have a nightcap.

"Vito, I enjoyed my evening as well. You are such a charming man. I can't remember the last time I've had this much fun. I was long overdue. I have just been working so hard that I haven't taken the time to relax and enjoy life."

"You have to learn to relax. You Americans work too much", as he held Monica's hand. Vito walked Monica to her hotel suite. They enjoyed brandy and more conversations. Vito held Monica in his arm as he enjoyed her curvaceous body. Monica enjoyed the touch of a man. She hadn't dated or been with anyone in almost 3 years. Vito kissed Monica's lips and savored the sweetness. Vito ignited Monica's passion and emotions she hadn't experienced in years. The two enjoyed the blissful moments as their gentle kisses turned intense, sexual, and engulfing. Monica and Vito made love as they explored each other's bodies. Both were satisfied as the two of them slipped into slumber.

Monica spent her remaining time with Vito. The two of them visited Milan and Tuscany. Vito wanted to show Monica so many things while she was in town. Her two weeks in Italy quickly ended.

"Vito I had a wonderful time in Italy. Will I ever see you again", as her eyes were slightly glazy.

"I don't know. Would you like to see me again? I would love to see you again if you will have me."

"Don't be silly. You know I want to see you again. I enjoyed my time with you so much", as she rubbed her finger gently over his nose and across his lips.

"I will continue to come to the US. I have business in the states. I can always come and check on my operations", as he smiled and kissed Monica before she left the car.

"I would really like that. I know you are a busy business-man, but if you will make time for me, I will do the same and make time for you", as she smiled. "I will call you when I land back in the states."

"Thank you."

Over the next six months, Vito continued to visit his US operations, but seeing Monica was his primary motivation for trip. Vito and Monica grew closer emotionally with each visit. Their personalities complimented each other. Also during that time, the couple took getaway trips all over the world. On his private jet, it wasn't uncommon for Vito to whisk Monica away to an exotic destination at a moment's notice. Some of the couple's getaway destinations included Puerto Rico, Dominica Republic, Mexico, and Brazil.

For the first time in years, Monica had a reason to live outside of her desire to run her real estate firm. Her business was doing well and she was in love. Something she hadn't experienced in a long time. In less than three years, emo-tionally, Monica was at a good point. She no longer felt over-whelmed, distressed, and abused.

With the economy recovering, Monica created new opportunities. Her business network expanded, referrals increased, and new business relationships grew. On one of

Vito's many visits, he mentioned to Monica that he was interested in buying a small wine distribution company based in Baltimore, Maryland. The distribution company, which had several warehouses that it owned, was a prime opportunity to expand his US operations.

Monica did some research and determined that one of Jonathan Westin's companies owned the wine distribution company. Monica seized the opportunity to serve as the transactional broker for both clients. Monica would broker the business purchase initially and then negotiate the leasing contracts separately. Under this structured arrangement, Vito would assume controlling financial interest while negotiations were ongoing for leasing and property management. The business operations phase of the purchase occurred quickly within three months.

Radiating with enthusiasm, Monica called Jonathan to notify him that she had a buyer for his problem stricken warehouses. She would facilitate the transfer of these dilapidated assets improving profitability for her client's portfolio.

"Jonathan, I know it's been a while since we last spoke. How are things", she vivaciously inquired.

"Things are going well. I'm keeping busy with new deals and opportunities, etc. How are things in with you? How is business?"

"Business is growing. I'm expanding operations along the East Coast. Personally, things couldn't be better", as she jubilantly replied. "The purpose of my call is to give you good news: I have a buyer for those problem warehouses we discussed almost a year ago. The buyer is a wine and spirits owner and is willing to accept the warehouses 'As Is'," Monica vibrantly proclaimed.

"That is good news. Send me the contract and I will personally take a look."

"I will send it right over to your office. I will talk to you soon", as she ended the call. Monica sent the document and Jon did review the contract.

True to his cynical and sinister personality, Jonathan wanted to find out more about this 'buyer' Monica was discussing. More importantly, why was she so cheerful? Monica demeanor was significantly different from his initial introduction. What was driving her cheerfulness? The buyer for the warehouses was: Li Volsi Ltd. Jonathan hired a private detective to gather information on Li Volsi Ltd and Monica. Jon wanted to know if there was a connection between the two. A few weeks later, Jon received a package with photographs from the investigation. The information confirmed his suspicions: Monica and Vito Li Volsi were personally involved. Jon was envious and furious as he gazed at the pictures of Monica and Vito. He vowed his vengeance toward Vito by stalling the warehouses purchase. Jon decided to take Vito's earnest deposit and stall the sale of the warehouses. Meanwhile, he would escalate the rental rates to exuberate levels during negotiations. If Vito didn't pay the rates, Jon would evict the distribution company, which would impact operations, and create negative publicity for Vito's company tainting the company's public image. Over the next few months, Jon would exercise his diabolical plan.

Meanwhile, Monica and Vito celebrated their initial victory of the purchase of the small distribution company with anticipation of the sale of the warehouses to occur soon. The couple flew to Bora, Bora to commemorate their recent win.

They spent a blissful week on the ivory beaches, devouring each other in animalistic lovemaking.

Upon returning, Monica continued to work the transaction for the sale of the warehouses. Over the coming months and as expected, Jonathan did execute his diabolical plan. Legal counsel for both parties quickly got involved; the situation escalated, and eventually both parties wound up in the court. Vito sued Jonathan for breach of contract and brand defamation. The courts ruled in Vito's favor. The courts ordered Jonathan to sell the warehouses at the agreed upon price, and punitive damages of $5 million dollars. As the two men were leaving the courtroom, they both stared each other down like two hunger wolves.

"Mr. Westin, did you think you could just take my money and extort more like a 'slum lord,'" as he repulsively snared at him. Vito's attorney held his arm in front of his client.

"It's ok. You, your wife, and your real estate whore can live happily ever after in those warehouses," as he walked away. The next day, Jonathan terminated his contractual agreement with Salazar Realty.

Although Vito and his wife had been separated for almost two years, legally, they were still married. They both decided to take some time apart to reevaluate their priorities. Vito had moved on emotionally and planned to file for divorce when the legal separation period reached one year under Italian law. For now, it was merely a matter of time. His wife, on the other hand, felt her husband was having an affair and the affair was the motivating factor for the separation. Unknowing to her, Vito wanted a separation because his wife often nagged and behaved immature. His wife was nineteen years his junior. Vito didn't meet Monica until after a few months into his legal separation period.

During the legal proceedings, leading up to the court case, Vito and Monica didn't see each other because of the tension and her fiduciary relationship in the real estate transaction. Monica was feeling physically unusual. She also realized that she had missed her menstrual cycle since her trip to Bora, Bora. Frightened and confused, she took a pregnancy test. Monica was pregnant. She never imagined this startling and horrifying scenario. Monica was 45 and had never been pregnant until now. She felt ashamed and humiliated. She was pregnant with a married man's child. Even though Vito was getting a divorce, Monica felt disgraceful that she had allowed herself to get involved in such a precarious situation. She was apprehensive in telling Vito in fear of his reaction. Eventually Monica called and requested to see Vito.

"Vito, when you will you be back in the states", she emotionally inquired.

"I am still in the US and will be here for a couple of more weeks. What is wrong?" he compassionately inquired.

"I need to see you. We need to talk."

"I will clear my calendar for tomorrow; is that soon enough?"

"Yes, tomorrow is fine," as tears streamed down her cheeks. Monica made an emergency appointment with her doctor to confirm her greatest fear. Monica's tests were conclusive. She was five weeks pregnant.

Vito, baffled and concerned, met Monica the next day.

"Monica what is the matter? Why are you upset?"

"Vito, I don't know how to say it."

"Say what?"

"I am pregnant", as she burst into tears.

"Really, you are?" as his eyes widened with surprise and excitement. Vito put his arm around her.

"I love you," he calmly responded. I am so excited. I am finally going to be a father. I always wanted children.

"This situation is all wrong", as she sobbed. "Vito, you are still married. What are you going to tell your wife?"

"I only have a few more months before I can file for divorce. I don't love her. I only married her because I wanted children. After we got married, she told me she couldn't have children because she had ovarian cancer years ago. I tolerated her for years but I always wanted children; something she could never give me."

"I am overwhelmed. This situation is just too much for me to deal with right now. I need some time," she emotionally responded.

"Baby, take whatever time you need. If you need anything, let me know." Vito had his driver drop Monica off at her house. Although Vito was excited, she still felt ashamed that she was unmarried and pregnant. She struggled with what her family would say. They would have so many questions. The more she thought about the situation, the more emotionally upset she became. Monica slipped into a depressed state of mind. She questioned every decision since her divorce. She lacked confident, expressed confusion, and felt devalued. All these negative emotions and stress took its toll on her body. The next day she went to see her doctor after showing signs of vaginal bleeding. Her doctor conducted some tests and determined that Monica had experienced a miscarriage. Monica spent a night in the hospital for observations and additional testing.

Monica gained enough emotional strength to call Vito.

"Vito, have you gotten back yet," as she sobbed.

"No, I haven't gotten back yet. We had mechanical difficulties over Maine and had to land to fix the problem."

"Are you ok?" as her focus shifted.

"Yes, I'm fine. Are you ok?"

"Vito, I lost the baby," she said with tears in her eyes.

"I'm so sorry", as tears filled his eyes. His heart sank. He wanted a child so badly. More importantly, Vito wanted a child with Monica. Vito directed the pilot to return to the US.

"I have to go. I can't talk right now."

"I am on my way back."

Over the next couple of days, Monica decided she couldn't see Vito anymore. Although she was in love with him, he was still a married man for now. That fact was more than she could handle.

"Monica, I just landed. Are you home? Can I come by?"

"Yes! We need to talk."

Vito arrived and had his driver drop him off at Monica's house. Vito and Monica sat in the living room and had a candid discussion.

"Vito, I can't see you anymore. This whole situation is all wrong. Although I am in love with you, I can't continue to see you", as tears streamed down her cheeks. "You are still married and as long as you are, we can't be together. I'm so sorry. I can't do this anymore."

"I won't try to change your mind. I am in love with you as well. I just wished things were different. When my divorce is final, will you re-consider?"

Vito, to be honest, I don't know how I will feel in six

months or however long it takes for things to be final. Right now, I can't continue the way things are; I am sorry", as she stopped sobbing.

"Good bye Vito", as she hugged and kissed him on the cheek.

"Good bye Monica", as he turned away glazy-eyed. Vito left and headed back to Italy. Days turned into months. However, Monica and Vito didn't speak again after the day he left her house. Heartbroken and devastated by Monica, Vito decided he didn't want to die a lonely old man. Vito withdrew his divorce paperwork and reconciled with his wife. In his heart, he loved Monica and always would.

CHAPTER 6

[PRESENT Day]
Lance's flight touched down Sunday evening at Dulles International Airport. The driver picked him up and dropped him at his hotel in Bethesda, Maryland. Lance settled into his suite and prepared his presentation for his upcoming meeting with Monica. Lance went to bed early. While reviewing his questions and rehearsing his presentation, Lance wondered about Monica personally. Although he dated women around his own age, he often considered mature women more compatible, zestful, with few inhibitions.

[I have to focus. This is a business meeting. I shouldn't even be thinking about her on a personal level. She is probably married, dating someone, or not interested in a younger man. I know DC has so many prominent and powerful men. This should be an interesting experience to say the least. The first and main order of business is to build a relationship. I need to make contact if I plan to pull this deal off.]

[Phone Rang]

"Hello."

"Hi, it's Candice. I just wanted to let you know I arrived here in Brazil safely. It's beautiful here. You should join me."

"I would love to join you. Unfortunately, I'm covered up with work. I have a critical meeting with a real estate contact in the DC area. I got in not long ago, and I'm preparing for my upcoming meeting tomorrow."

"You want me to let you go?"

"No, I have a few minutes. Besides, I welcome the break. I have been working non-stop since I saw you in Chicago. Between running my company and getting this real estate deal off the ground, I'm swamped."

"You need a vacation. You have to get away some-times to recharge your battery. We could lay on the beach and you could teach me how to become a business mogul like yourself."

"You are amusing, but you do have a valid point. I can't remember the last time I took a vacation. It seems like I go from one project to the next. I know I need to live a little. Perhaps when this deal is done, I will take some time and 'cool my jets.' However, right now, I will be working to make things happen."

"Handle your business. Just remember the little people!"

"More jokes I see."

"Seriously, I just wanted to let you know I arrived safely and wanted to hear your voice. I know you are busy. I will give you a call when I get back to the states."

"That sounds good. I will talk to you soon."

The next morning, Lance arrived at Monica's Bethesda-based corporate office. He checked in with the receptionist as she notified Monica that Lance had arrived. Monica's recep-tionist was slender, blonde, and very attractive. She took note of the tall dark haired handsome man that showed up at the office early Monday morning. She continued to work but discretely admired the well-dressed man. Her imagination ran wild as she envisioned him leaning over the desk to kiss her tender lips. She could see herself running her fingers through his ebony hair as she savored his lips touching hers.

Moments later, Monica came out her office to meet Lance Howard.

"Hello Lance, Monica Salazar. Please to finally meet you."

"Lance Howard, the pleasure is all mine."

"Come into my office. Would you like anything to drink like water or coffee?"

"Thanks. I'm fine. I'm trying to get used to this East Coast weather. The humidity is vastly different from California."

"I can imagine. I have been to the West Coast a few times. I love the weather out there but I'm an East Coast kind of woman", she laughed as the two of them sat at the table in her office.

Monica was always well dressed. She adopted that value from her upbringing. Her parents always told her to look like she was going to a job interview every day because she never knew when she may meet that person she may need to impress. Today was no exception. Monica had on her tailored navy blue two-piece skirt set with a champagne colored, low cut blouse that accentuated her voluptuous breasts. Lance tried to maintain his poise during the meeting. However, his eyes drifted to her luscious breasts right in front of him. He admired her curvaceous figure for a woman in her mid-forties.

After the small talk, Monica got down to business. She didn't become a successful woman by wasting valuable time.

"So how have things been going since our meeting with Thomas?" Do you have any investors committed yet? What about the land associated with building a stadium? A large tract of land like that is not easy to find in the DC area. Besides, you are going to need some political connections to get a sport arena initiative passed", as her eyes rolled with skepticism.

"Monica, I have two investors committed to the deal in writing. I have another meeting with a prominent investor as well. It's scheduled in the next couple of weeks. As for the land, I will need your assistance in locating the land and some local financial institutions. I have a line of credit but my preference is to finance the land purchase through local lenders to build a relationship on the East Coast."

"I'm impressed", as her eyebrows raised with surprise. "I didn't think you had it in you actually", as she sighed and sucked her teeth, leaned back in her oversized leather chair.

"Oh you didn't think I could do it because I'm young?"

"No, I didn't think you could do it because you are inexperienced."

"Don't let my age fool you. I have been successful. I raised a lot of capital and took my company public. This isn't my first rodeo. I may not know all there is to know about real estate, but I do know and understand business", as he sat forward-looking Monica directly in the eye.

"Well, there is no need to get defensive. Business is about relationships. I have built my business on relationships. Hopefully, this will be the beginning of our business relationship." Monica was excellent at conflict diffusion and conflict resolution. In her line of business, managing personalities was a requirement involving finesse and skill.

Lance sat back in his chair as Monica sat back in her chair crossing her legs. The tension was high between the two.

"Monica, since I will be doing business here on the East Coast, I am in the market for a condo. I don't want to do yard work, but I want the convenience of the normal amenities. I know this DC traffic is brutal. Would that be something you would be able to help me find?"

"Traffic is easy to find. It's everywhere. Now a house, I can have one of my agents pull some listings. What price range are you looking at staying within?

"I want something nice. Besides, I thought you would be able to show me some listings. That is unless you are too important to show me properties", as he smiled flashing those radiating teeth. Monica eyes rolled as she shook her head.

"Is this how you behave with your new business acquaintance? I'm going to tell Thomas how you treated me when I came to DC to meet you in person", as he cracked a smug smile on his face.

"How long are you in town?"

"I will be here a few days. Why, are you going to show me some properties while I'm in town?"

"Perhaps I can show a few."

The next day, Monica called Lance to let him know she had found a few prospective properties for him to view. Monica never wasted time when it came to the real estate business. She knew time was money and if she didn't move assertively, then she could possibly lose a prospective client to another agent.

"Hello Lance. Did I wake you?"

"No, I'm an early riser. Besides, I like to get my workout done in the mornings before I start my day. What's up?"

"I have pulled the listings for a few properties. Two are

in Bethesda, which is not far from my office, and the other two are in Potomac. Do you prefer Maryland or are you open to living in Virginia as well? I meant to ask you before I pulled the listings."

"I'm flexible, but I know the taxes in Virginia are kind of high: I pay enough taxes in California to last three lifetimes."

Monica laughed at the taxes comment.

"I didn't know you laughed. I thought that was some strange anomaly. Is this year a leap year?"

"I see you have jokes. I laugh often and long, but I take my business relationships very seriously."

"I can tell. I didn't see you as an easygoing person. You seem very focused and intense. I know you don't know me, but it would be nice since we will be working together to as least become a little better acquainted."

"I don't mind having a cordial conversation. We can talk more when I pick you up. How soon will you be ready and what's the address to your hotel?"

"I'm ready now so you can come by: 23300 Wisconsin Avenue."

"That sounds good. I will be there in about 20 minutes", as Monica ended the call. She grabbed the listings. Looked in the mirror, adjusted her clothes and makeup before heading to her car.

Approximately 20 minutes later, Monica arrived at Lance's hotel, picked him up and they headed to their first property. It was only 10 minutes away from Lance's hotel.

"This is close to where I'm staying. It must be a nice area. I'm not that familiar with the DC area. I have only been here a few times for business, and I didn't get to see much when I visited."

"It's not a bad place to live. A lot of people come here for work and end up staying. The traffic can get really hectic sometimes if you have to get on the beltway."

"I have heard of that beltway traffic. I know California has traffic, but it's nowhere near as congested as here. Where do you live?"

"I live here in Bethesda. There are several nice homes in the area but I know you mentioned that you wanted a condo."

"Yes, I don't do lawn work, and I don't want to start at this point", as he rolled his eyes and shook his head.

"I see", as she exhaled deeply, turned and walked around the condo. The developer built this condo approximately seven years ago. It has all the normal amenities: granite countertops, gas fireplace, carpet, oversized closets, etc."

"Does it come furnished?"

"This particular one does. Some are not furnished. What is your preference?"

"I would like one already furnished. Since I will be here mostly for business, I don't want the hassle of shopping for furniture. I like shopping but not for furniture."

"Keep this one in mind. We are heading to the next couple of properties in Bethesda before we go to Potomac."

Lance and Monica headed to the other two condos before going to Potomac. The developer built this condo three years ago. This particular condo is one of the last three remaining from the development. Monica showed Lance the largest of the three condos. The other two were too small.

"Monica, how long you been in the real estate business?" as they strolled around the last condo.

"I have been in the business over 23 years now. Why do you ask?"

"I was curious. You seem well versed in all the aspects of the industry. Thomas mentioned you were the person to know regarding real estate in the DC area. I can see why he would say those things. I'm impressed", as he looked out the window at the view.

"Did I hear you correctly? Did you say you were impressed? I better write this down. [Captain's log: Star date 230145, I'm here in Bethesda, Maryland with Lance Howard, and he acknowledged that he was impressed with my savviness in the real estate industry]."

"Oh my! Now look at who has jokes. I didn't think you had those in you."

"Don't be fooled. I'm very friendly and amicable."

"Really, are we talking about the same person? You wanted to 'tear my head off' in the office just yesterday."

"I don't know what you are talking about. It must be your imagination. I'm angelic. It must have been my evil twin," as she gestured a halo above her head."

"I may be young but that doesn't mean I'm naïve, but it sounded good", as Lance laughed and shook his head.

"Speaking of age, I know I'm not supposed to ask, but how old are you (age range)?"

"Didn't your mother teach you to never ask a woman her age? I'm over 21 a few times over."

"You aren't going to tell me are you?"

"That would be a no. Perhaps if you be nice, play well with others and be a good citizen, one day I may share."

"OK!"

"On a different note, what did you think about the condos we saw today?

"Well they were all nice. I like the last one in Potomac. What was the price of that one again?"

"It's listed at $1.2 million, but I believe there is some room to negotiate. It's been on the market for a while and the market is soft right now for condos in the Potomac area. Most people purchase single family homes in this area."

"Let me give it some thought. I will follow up with you soon. I have to get back to California to prepare for an upcoming trip to Brazil to meet with another investor."

Lance and Monica made eye contact, shook hands, and departed ways at Lance's hotel.

CHAPTER 7

L ANCE headed back to California to prepare for his upcoming trip to Brazil. He was looking forward to meeting Lucas Cardoso. Lucas seemed like a friendly businessman but looks may be deceiving. Lucas and Jonathan friendship could mean anything considering Lance's "hot-cold" relationship with the venture capitalist billionaire. Although Jon presented an image of helpfulness, Lance had his suspicions. He couldn't confirm anything but his intuition caused him to think. For now, he would continue to monitor the situation and see how things unfolded.

Lance had several emails and phone calls to catch up on during his trip back to the West Coast. He read through his emails from his executive team responding promptly as needed. The project for his new software product line was on schedule. This new software had excellent market capitalization potential. Lance's products had achieved a whopping twenty-two percent of the market share from other well-established organizations. Lance continued to maintain situational awareness of the progress of this new project. If this project proved successful, he would soon move into a commanding position in the video sharing segment, especially within the social media market.

Lance gave Lucas a quick call to confirm his meeting in a week.

"Lucas, how are you. I wanted to reach out to confirm our meeting next week."

"Lance, it's good to hear from you. How are things on your end? How is the weather in California?"

"The weather is great. I was on the East Coast for the last few days but I'm back now. I'm sure the weather there is very nice."

"You are correct. You will see when you get down here. By the way, my calendar is free for next week. I wanted to make sure I had availability. I will show you around my country. Perhaps you will give up the States and come down where we laugh, live, and enjoy life."

"I am looking forward to my trip. I have never been there so this trip should be interesting."

"It will be Lance. I will show you a really good time; not viewing the country through your typical tourist's eyes."

Lance ended his call with Lucas. He noticed that Brazilians spend time talking about other topics before getting down to business. This was something he had to get used to doing. Jon told him to keep that in mind when talking to Lucas.

[Phone Rang]

"Hey Lance, This is Candice."

"Hey, how are you? Why do you always say your name? I have your number programmed into my phone", as he laughed, shook his head, and rolled his eyes.

"Well, I know you are such a popular guy, and I'm sure you have so many women calling that you ask everyone to identify themselves," as she laughed.

"You are too much as always. How was your trip?"

"It was amazing. I could have stayed another week, but I had to get back to work. Otherwise, I may have moved down there. The weather is fabulous and the people are so warm, nice, and friendly. They love to party too."

"That sounds like fun. I have a business meeting in Brazil next week. I'm really looking forward my trip. I have never been there, so I'm looking forward to the trip."

"You will have a great time. I just wanted to give you a quick call to let you know I am back in LA and that I had a good time. Give me a call when you get back from your trip. I would love to see you again. I'm still smiling from Chicago", as she twirled her hair.

"I definitely will give you a call when I get back", as he rubbed his fingers through his hair and thought back to Chicago.

Lance's flight touched down in Rio late in the evening of the following week. Lucas had arranged for a car to pick him up at the airport. It was about a 20-minute drive from the airport to Lucas's estate right outside of Rio.

Lucas met him at the front door.

"Welcome to Brazil. How was your flight?"

"It was a good flight down. There was very little turbulence so I kicked back and relaxed."

"That sounds good. I am sure you are probably tired. I will let you relax and we will reconnect in the morning. Brunch is usually around 10-11am but I can always have my chef make you a Brazilian special", as he spoke in Portuguese to one of his staff to get Lance's bags.

The next morning, Lance woke to the tweeting sounds of birds, and running water. As he looked out the back window of his bedroom, he saw the water fountain statue of a woman with a downward turned vase. Water was flowing from the vase into the open pond. There was a marble staircase leading from the patio overlooking the plush green and well-manicured lawn. In the far background was a gigantic monumental rock protruding upward breaking up the blue skyline extending across the horizon. All along the 50 acre, estate were tropical banana palms, trees and other thick but beautifully spaced vegetation.

Lance wondered his way down the hall into the open and spacious family living area. The area was right off the large kitchen. In his mind, the architect designed the house with entertainment and family gatherings in mind.

He saw Lucas in the family living area sitting in what looked like his favorite chair.

"Lance, I see you are awake. How did you rest? Was everything ok in your guest suite?"

"Yes, everything was fine. I actually got a good night sleep. I usually don't sleep late. I guess I was tired. I have been on the run a lot lately."

"I understand. You are in Brazil. You have to relax. Today, I will show you around Rio. I think you will enjoy a break from the fast pace life of the states," as he nodded his head.

"That would be very hospitable. I am looking forward to seeing some of the country."

"Then it is settled. After you eat, we will go into the city. My wife and daughter have already left to go shopping. Now, it's time for the men to get out and enjoy some of the sites."

After brunch, the two men departed for the city to enjoy the sites of Rio. Lance was experiencing a different world.

The people of Brazil were friendly as they enjoyed life. Lucas took Lance to some of the popular tourist attractions as well as some places less traveled by the commercial tourist's crowd.

* * *

Jon called Charlene Brooks. He hadn't spoken to her in a long time. Charlene was a prominent businesswoman based in the Los Angeles area. She had served as a venture capitalist early in her career but now she primarily sat on several boards in order to help companies continue growing their businesses and providing solid directions.

"Hey Charlie, how are you these days," spoken in his deep, slightly abrasive voice.

"Hey Jon, what do you want," she replied in a slightly hostile defensive tone as her eyes rolled.

"Is that any way to treat the guy that helped you get into the venture capitalism business? I was your mentor. I helped you a lot, didn't I?"

"Jon, you usually help yourself. What is your point?"

"I will be in town in a couple of days. I have some business and I was wondering if I could see you. It has been a long time. I would like to take you to dinner."

"Let me think about it. I will get back to you," she sharply replied.

"Okay. If you do decide, here is my cell number", as he politely gave her his number.

Charlene exhaled loudly. I wonder what Jon wants now. Maybe he does want to see me. Perhaps he had changed. I will have to think about it.

Later that evening, Charlene called Jon. "What day will

you be in town? I'm a busy woman so I need to know if I have some availability."

"I will be in town Friday morning. I have some meetings, but I should be free by early afternoon. Perhaps we can go to dinner on Saturday."

"Oh wow. I'm surprise you can fit me in on a prime date night like Saturday."

"Why do you continue to say mean things to me? You hurt my feelings."

"You don't have feelings!"

"Touché!" as he retracted his victimizing tone. "I will see you on Saturday. Do you have a preference on where you would like to go?"

"I will make the reservation. I will let you know where we are going when you arrive."

"That sounds good. I will talk to you on Friday."

Jon contacted his assistant to coordinate his travel arrangements. The next day he arrived in LA on his private jet for his early meetings. After concluding his business meetings, he visited one of his favorite private clubs to relax for the afternoon. As he was sipping on his favorite cognac and enjoying his Cuban cigar, he made a phone call.

"Lucas, how are things going? Is everything going according to plan?"

"Yes, everything is going according to plan. We are out touring Rio now. I will keep you posted."

"Thanks, I will talk to you soon", as he ended the call.

"Another drink Mr. Westin," the cocktail waitress replied.

"No, I will be leaving shortly after I finish this one."

Charlene did her normal Saturday routine, which

included time at the spa and salon. Although she has known Jonathan for years, she was always excited to see him. She just didn't want him to know how much she enjoys his company. She saw his brash masculine tone as a turn-on because he was such a powerful man.

Jonathan had his driver pick up Charlene from her house. Jonathan didn't drive much unless it was one of his sports cars. Shortly after arrival at the restaurant, Jon and Charlene took their seats. The restaurant was one of the most exclusive restaurants in LA.

Jonathan proposed a toast: to old friends and lasting relationships. The two of them laughed, enjoyed their meals, and appreciated the service. Jon left a generous tip. The couple departed as the driver whist them away.

"I had fun as always. You know how to show a woman a good time: great food, wine, and conversation," as she laughed. Charlene never could hold her liquor. "Would you like to come in for a nightcap?"

"Yes, I will come in for a little while", as he gestured to the driver to head out for the evening.

As soon as Jon walked through the door, Charlene jumped him and started aggressively kissing him, as she took off his tie and shirt—ripping the buttons from his shirt. The passion was always intense between the two of them. Perhaps, the tension was the turn-on for Charlene. Jon knew where to touch her to get an electric reaction.

Right now, there were no tender moments. It was intense, animalistic passion. Charlie knew what she wanted and Jon knew how to give it to her. Within seconds, she had slipped out of her dress exposing her toned, slender body. For a woman in her forties, Charlie was in excellent shape.

She had the looks of a thirty year old, but the experience of a lifetime when it came to sex.

Charlie dropped to her knees as gave Jon unfounded pleasure by licking the inside of his thigh grabbing his manhood with one hand and gripping Jon's ass with her other. She looked up at him as she gave him pleasure licking the tip of his staff with her tantalizing tongue. Jon leaned back as he grabbed her hair pushing her down on his member until he could hear her gagging. Charlie stood up and licked Jon's chest. He turned her around and bent her over the counter in the kitchen. Charlie arched her back as she grabbed the edge of the counter. Jon squeezed her nipples as he licked the back of her neck. Aggressively, he grabbed a handful of her long brown hair as he slid inside of her. She moaned as if he had taken her breath away. She whispered as he went deep inside and then pulled out.

"What the fuck. Don't tease me," she huskily replied.

"I'm punishing you."

"Why! What did I do?"

"I am punishing you for not saying immediately that you wanted to see me", as he slid back inside of her. She arched her back even more this time in order to feel him deep inside of her. Jon pumped her vigorously as he pulled her hair and spanked her ass. She uttered and moaned with each animalistic hump. Charlie was creamy and throbbing as she continued to hold onto the counter. She looked back and tried to kiss him, but Jon forced Charlie to look forward pushing her face down on the counter. He pumped her more until her entire body grew tense.

"I'm going to finish you in your bedroom", as he suddenly stopped just as Charlie was approaching her first climatic milestone.

Just as he had promised, Jon continued to pump Charlie

intensely until her body erupted in pure pleasure of release. Jon continued pumping her until he could feel the pressure building and suddenly he erupted inside of her with his manly release. Charlie moaned and reached another climatic milestone as Jon passionate liquid continued to flow inside of her pond of passion.

The next morning as the two of them were lying in bed cuddling, they began to talk.

"You were incredibly hot last night. What brought that on?"

"It was the alcohol", as she grinned. "No seriously, it's been a while since I had good sex. Besides, you know my body so well. My pussy really responds to you for whatever reason", as her eyes rolled when she looked at him.

"I can tell. So what is going on in your world? What interesting things have you been working on lately? Have you joined any new company boards?"

"I have been busy. I have joined a few new boards. Most of the companies are tech startups."

"That's interesting. Any good products or are they mostly fluff and a passing fad?"

"There is one new company I think may have potential. It's a video sharing company. I think this company has long-term potential within the social media community. The founder is Lance Howard. Have you met him?"

"No, that name doesn't sound familiar", as he looked out the window.

"Well the company has a new software product line they are working on that should hit the market in the next six months. The company is extremely undervalued but will soar once this new product hits the market."

"So do I need to break out my checkbook", as he gave Charlie a grin.

"Yes, but you know I am not supposed to share insider information," as she laughed and gave Jon a kiss on the cheek.

"Your secret is safe with me", as he put his finger over his lips.

"That is enough corporate business; now I need you to come here and take care of some other business underneath the covers", as she rolled on top of him.

* * *

Monica continued to search for feasible sites consisting of approximately of 100 acres. This was no easy task in the DC area considering how scarce and valuable land was surrounding the District. There were a couple of feasible options but both areas were too far from the general population or there were zoning constraints. She continued to search to find a viable option to present to her client.

Monica also began socializing the idea of a soccer stadium/sports complex to her political contacts. Charles Franklin was the first name to come to mind. Charles was a Senator for the state of Maryland. His re-election campaign had faced some challenges in the past, but currently didn't display any immediate threats as the sitting incumbent. Funding was always a challenge and presently his political climate was no different. He needed a big donor to help him win comfortably.

Monica had known Charles for years. She had supported his campaigns and often referred key donors in his direction when she saw their efforts could benefit from having Charles as a political ally.

"Hello, Senator Franklin, how are you these days?"

"Monica Salazar, what did I do right to owe this call," as he gestured his aide to leave his office and give him some privacy.

"Senator, I know it's been a while since we last spoke," she replied. I wanted to see if you are available to meet this week. Will that be possible?"

"Monica, let me take a look at my calendar. I will move some things around, but a meeting this week seems doable." Senator Franklin's assistant checked his schedule and was able to work out an hour meeting in his office on Capitol Hill. With an upcoming re-election, Senator Franklin was very flexible when it came to funding his campaign.

The following week Monica met Charles in his office to discuss her proposal. Charles was surprised Monica wanted to meet with him.

"Monica, it's good to see you as always. You are getting younger and younger every time I see you."

"I see you haven't changed a bit. You are always flirting with me."

"Well at least I am consistent. Besides, if it wasn't for my political office, the public spotlight, and a minor technicality of being married, I would pursue you."

"Have you been taking your medicine Senator? I see you are still delusional", they both laughed.

"Seriously Monica, why did you want to meet with me so soon?"

"I have a prospective donor to your campaign. He is interested in supporting your cause and fostering your long track record."

"Bullshit. You and I both know that is not how this game is played in this town", as he cracked a smug grin.

"My associate is looking at bringing a soccer franchise with a soccer stadium to the area. His consortium is looking for legislative support as well as some tax incentives for the first five years. If you noticed, I didn't say the investment group would need funding support did I?"

"Monica, you are right. I'm listening", as he sat back in his oversized leather chair and crossed his legs.

"I won't go into the details, but I wanted to run the idea by you first. I would like for you to socialize the idea with some of your trusted colleagues to get a 'feel' for support but more importantly, strong opposition."

"I will do that and get back to you. So when are we going on that dinner date", as he rubbed his hands together in anticipation.

"Charles, stop dreaming", as her eyes rolled and she shook her head. The two of them shook hands as Monica thanked him for his time. Monica had planted the idea in the Senator's head. The rest was up to him, and he knew just what to do.

* * *

Lance enjoyed the various sites and attractions in Brazil. Lance felt there was so much to see. The weather was mild like Southern California, but the ambience of Rio was appealing on so many levels.

"Lucas, you really know how to show a man a good time. You are an excellent host. The food and wine has been exquisite. Just when I thought you couldn't impress me more, you take me to another locale that is overwhelmingly a surprise."

"Lance, I'm glad you are enjoying. Rio has so much to offer. I have been all over the world, but I find myself coming back to my home country. Tomorrow night, my wife Elena will prepare a family dinner. Even with all our house staff, she still enjoys cooking at least once when we have guest in town."

Elena always enjoyed cooking the family meal before the houseguest departed. It was Brazilian tradition to send the guests off with good food and good wine before they traveled. Elena went shopping early that morning with her daughter Amelia. They went into town to purchase fresh fruits and vegetables in preparation for the festive meal.

Later that afternoon, Lucas and Lance had a meeting in the study. It was the perfect time to discuss the real reason for his trip.

"Lance, I hope you have enjoyed your time here in Brazil. At this point we can discuss your business proposal", as Lucas sat back in his chair. Lance got the formality of the NDA out of the way and began his presentation.

[The market in Washington DC area is prime to support a soccer stadium with the demographics, and income. There was a preliminary proposal a couple of years ago but the developer couldn't raise adequate capital to fund the project and sustain the franchise. The preliminary figures for the land and construction are $480 million with an additional $200 million payroll and operations budget for the franchise. I will be the lead investor with my $100 million equity overseeing the project from DC. I have identified and met with the owner of a real estate brokerage firm that has the capacity and the network to undertake a project of this magnitude. I am seeking investors to collaborate with to own the land and a soccer team franchise in the DC area. Does that sound like something of interest to you?]

"Lance, I have a couple of questions. What about ROI and what is the timeframe?"

"With the land, my team estimated the capitalization rate of 12 percent. From a franchising perspective, payroll would be high the first two years of operations but would have a downward vector as personnel and athletes come under contract. The projected return on investment is 8 percent after year two in my financial model after completion of construction. I can provide you the prospectus along with financials for your team to review. We can reconnect in a couple of weeks if you are interested in investing in the project."

"That sounds reasonable and fair. Here is my business card; you can send the encrypted information over to my executive team", as Lucas handed him his business card placed between two fingers.

"Thank you for your time and hospitality", as Lance shook Lucas's hand.

"No problem. Now that we have concluded our business, let's continue to enjoy the festivities of Rio. My wife is excited about the meal tonight", as Lucas raised his wine glass.

As the two men departed into downtown Rio, Lucas's wife arrived back at the estate to begin cooking. Amelia joined her mother in preparing the meal. Amelia's brother, Bernardo, returned from the beach. Bernardo was a recent law school graduate. All of Lucas's family would be at the dinner tonight.

The house staff set the table with the food arranged in the center. It was a round mahogany table with heavy wooden chairs. Lance made his way down to the formal dining area. Everyone had arrived and was talking between himself and herself. Lucas voice gained the attention of the room.

"Everyone, I want you to welcome our guest Lance Howard from California," as he introduced him to his wife, his son, and finally his daughter. Lance thought Lucas's daughter was the most beautiful woman he had ever seen. Her long brown hair, brown eyes, bronze colored skin, and curvaceous figure captivated Lance with her every movement. Lance knew he could not stare for obvious reasons but struggled nonetheless. Amelia found Lance interesting as well. Normally her father's guests were old married businessmen. For a change, here was a tall, dark haired charming man that had been a guest in the house, and she didn't even know it. Their paths had not cross during the days since Lance's arrival until now.

Because her father was a well-known and powerful man in Rio, most men were too intimidated to approach her. Although her father was charming and friendly, most people knew he was very temperamental when it came to his daughter.

The food was delectable and the wine was exquisite as everyone enjoyed the culinary skills of Elena. Amelia sat across the table from Lance taking any opportunity she could; gazing discreetly at him. Her imagination ran wild as she imagined him kissing her out by the pool or the two of them sharing a moment admiring the sunset. She could see herself running her fingers through his ebony hair, and him pulling her closer with those big arms and broad shoulders of his.

Lucas proposed the final toast for the evening before everyone adjourned to his or her respective areas. Lance took a walk out by the pool. He enjoyed the nightscape of the lights reflecting against the jade colored pool. Amelia retired to her suite, but she caught a glimpse of Lance by the pool. She continued to savor in the tantalizing imagination of being intimately involved with Lance. Although she barely knew him, she could sense his calming spirit. She saw this as the perfect opportunity to have an intimate conversation. Amelia left her suite and ventured to enjoy the water.

"Hello, it's a nice night out isn't it?" she spoke in English with a strong Portuguese accent.

"Yes it is", as Lance turned around to confirm what he already knew: it was Amelia.

"So how has your trip to Brazil been so far?" she inquired curiously.

"It's been great. Your father has been an excellent host. He took me to see so many sites in the city. Rio has a lot to offer. Everyone here is so friendly."

"Yes, I have lived here my whole life. The area is fun, but I want to see other parts of the world. I always wanted to go to California. Where do you live?"

"I live in San Jose, California. It's not too far from Los Angeles. It's green, but not like here", as Lance couldn't keep his eyes off of Amelia.

"Are you single?" she inquired curiously.

"Yes", as Lance cracked a smile. "Are you single", as his eyebrows raised?

"I'm curious. Most of my father's guests are old married men. Most of the local men are intimidated by my father's position in the community, so I'm at a loss."

"I do understand. So do you go out in Rio?"

"Do you mean clubbing," she replied confusingly. Lance nodded.

"Yes, but not that often. I'm long overdue", as she laughed.

"You have a really beautiful smile", as she flashed her pearly white teeth at Lance.

"Thank you. Would you like to go out clubbing? I know my Father has been showing you around, but my father doesn't do clubs", as she giggled.

"Sure, I would love to see some of the night life for young professional adults."

"Then let me make a few calls and get a driver. It's better that way for safety and if we drink", as she winked. Here is my number. I will give you a call when it's time to go in about an hour. Is that ok?"

"That works for me. See you soon", as he gave her a slight wave.

Approximately an hour later, the two of them met the driver in front and out they went. Amelia took Lance to a couple of progressive but classy nightclubs. They danced, drank, and had an enjoyable time. They laughed as they danced most of the night away. At around 3am, they decided it was time to head back because Lance had a flight the next day. Lance walked Amelia to her suite. The couple talked about the adventurous time they had.

"Come to my room", as the two made eye contact.

"I don't know if that is a good idea. Although your Father is on the other end of the estate, I wouldn't want to disrespect his hospitality." Amelia put her fingers over Lance's mouth, pulled him inside her suite, and kissed him. Lance pulled her close as his large hands wrapped around her curvy frame. He could feel her breathing heavily as her soft hands traced over his broad shoulders. Her tongue teased his mouth and explored uncontrollably.

"I just wanted a kiss. I know my Father is not far away. I wouldn't disrespect my Father's house. I would like to visit Los Angeles. Will you meet me there?" as she rubbed over his face.

"Yes, I would love that as well. I can show you some of LA's 'hot' spots", as he ran his fingers through her hair as he rubbed down her shoulders. I better go. I will call you in the morning before I leave."

"I would like that", as she gave him another short kiss goodnight.

Sinful thoughts of Lance dominated her imagination. Kissing Lance left her both simmering and tingly as her thoughts galloped down the road to ecstasy. Her nipples were rigid as if a frigid wind had blown over them. Her fleshy, hairy pussy was throbbing as her womanly nectar flowed like molasses over raspberries. Her pink button of pleasure was ripe for the picking. Amelia's entire body ached as the smoldering ashes of desire engulfed her mind as she stuck her fingers inside her wet pussy and then sucked her fingers.

Lance went back to his suite, showered, and went to bed. He couldn't help but think about Amelia's curves, her tender lips, and her captivating hazel colored eyes. Although he was respectful of Lucas's Brazilian hospitality, Lance couldn't help but imagine a naughty and passionate encounter with Lucas's daughter. In his mind, kissing her lips was but a tease of a Brazilian treat of Brigadeiro. Lance soon drifted off to sleep with Amelia's luscious lips, long slender legs, bronze colored skin, and hazel colored eyes deeply imprinted upon his mind's eye.

In the serene and still of the summer night, Lance slept peacefully on his back drifting countlessly in and out of consciousness as his sexual desires of Amelia galloped. His thoughts continued in a loop of passion about Amelia's sleek legs folded as she dug her fingernails into his chests, riding the Italian stallion in a race to a climatic finish. The dream seemed surreal with vivid details. Lance could see her face as she gentle rocked back and forth on his stick of pleasure; arching her back with each manly thrust. Lance opened his eyes and realized that his dream was not a dream at all. Amelia had quietly creeped into Lance's suite, removed the covers from his brawny body, and devour him like prey. She had mounted Lance in an effort to tame the Italian stallion that had wondered into her Brazilian stable.

Amelia covered Lance's mouth before he could utter a word. She kissed him with her allusive tongue teasing Lance's mouth with each gliding swirl. She rocked back and forth gyrating up and down on his hard staff. The faster she bounced up and down, the more her pink cave throbbed. Amelia pounced deep on his rigid staff of pleasure. Lance well-endowed cock touched the top as she grinded deeply with each round and round motion. Soon, she gyrated faster as she approached the climatic finish line. Lance had the wood for the fire but not the fireplace but he knew she was smoking. He also knew that he could put out the flames of her raging intimate desires. Lance squeezed her protruding nipples as he held on to this scandalous Brazilian ride. Moments later, Amelia reached that climatic cliff as she rode uncontrollably. Lance shot his hot load deep inside of her as he arched his head back. She whimpered as the aftershocks of her orgasmic episode continued. She draped her exhausted but relaxed body over Lance as she struggled to catch her breath. Seconds later, she rolled off of the exotic Italian stud feeling a sense of conquest. There were two winners and no losers in this race of ecstasy.

"I would love to stay in your bed but it will be daylight soon," she whispered in his ear.

"I know but I'm glad you came", as the two kissed.

"I am too; in more ways than one." Amelia dressed in her robe and cautiously existed Lance's suite.

Chapter 8

M ONICA was concerned that the lucrative deal that
had "fallen" in her lap may fall apart. Although she
wasn't sure if Lance could pull this deal together, she knew
she had to do something. Reluctantly, she called the only
person she knew who had the means to make this deal
happen. Monica called Vito Li Volsi. Vito was the chairman
and major owner of his family's spirits empire. He was a
third generation owner of the empire with an estimated net
worth around 8 billion dollars.

"Hello, may I speak to Vito Li Volsi."

"Who is calling please," a woman responded in a strong
Italian-English voice.

"Tell him Monica Salazar from Washington DC."
Moments later, the woman returned to the line and indicated to hold for the connection.

"Hello, this is Vito. I didn't expect to hear from you
again. I am totally surprised you called. What do I owe
this privilege?"

"I have a business associate that will be reaching out
to you in the next few days. He has a proposal you may be
interested in considering."

"What type of proposal? Do you need money? I can send you money," he responded in an accommodating tone.

"Vito, I can't accept your money and we both know why," Monica replied reluctantly. "I know I said I wouldn't call you but things have changed. This is a career changing opportunity for me and you were the only person I knew that may be able to help."

"I understand."

"His name is Lance Howard. I have to go. I will talk to you another time", as she hung up the phone with tears in her eyes.

Monica called Lance to pass the information she had for a prospective investor. She indicated that Vito was very wealthy and that he loved soccer. However, she told Lance that he had to travel to Italy to meet him and pitch his prospectus. Lance had the passion. He was willing to do whatever necessary to make this land deal happen.

Lance called Vito's office to make an appointment. He then booked his flight. Lance arrived in Rome, Italy a few weeks later for his appointment. Vito's receptionist greeted Lance when he arrived.

"Lance Howard, my name is Vito Li Volsi; pleased to meet you." Vito was a large framed half-bald man. He had dark olive colored skin. Vito was in his late fifties. He loved to eat and it showed. Vito stood over six feet tall.

The two men got the normal pleasantries out of the way and soon got down to business.

"Monica tells me you have a business proposal that I may be interested in pursuing."

"Yes, it involves investing in a soccer franchise in the Washington DC area.

[The market in Washington DC area is prime to support a soccer stadium with the demographics, and income. There was a preliminary proposal a couple of years ago but the developer couldn't raise adequate capital to fund the project and sustain the franchise. The preliminary figures for the land and construction are $480 million with an additional $200 million payroll and operations budget for the franchise. I will be the lead investor with my $100 million equity overseeing the project from DC. I have identified and met with the owner of a real estate brokerage firm that has the capacity and the network to undertake a project of this magnitude. I am seeking investors to collaborate with to own the land and a soccer team franchise in the DC area. "With the land, my team estimated the capitalization rate of 12 percent. From a franchising perspective, payroll would be high the first two years of operations but would have a downward vector as personnel and athletes come under contract. The projected return on investment is 8 percent after year two in my financial model after completion of construction.]

"Lance, I want to thank you for your presentation. However, the numbers don't look lucrative enough for me to invest in at this time. Good luck in your venture. You remind me of me when I was your age," as he sat back in his chair and smoked a cigar.

"Thank you for your time. I can provide you with the financials if you reconsider", as Lance responded disappointedly.

"Yes, go ahead and leave a copy of the projections with my receptionist. If I change my mind, I have your contact information."

Lance left Vito's office extremely disappointed but

understood that rejection was part of the business venture process. That fact didn't take away the sting of traveling all the way to Italy and then having to return 'empty handed.' Lance took advantage of the opportunity by going site seeing. He visited some historical sites around Rome. Lance decided he would travel to Milan to check out some of the latest fashions. Milan was infamous for having the leading designs of the fashion world. Cutting edge design boutiques filled the city. It was a shopper's dream. Lance found his way around the strip stores. There were tailors that were making suits with delivery times within a week. The competition was fierce. Since he didn't have time, he decided to buy a nice suit off the rack. After he purchased his suit and left the store, he accidently ran into a very attractive woman. She appeared to be in her late 30s or early 40s.

"I'm sorry, pardon me. It was clearly my fault," the woman responded in a strong Italian accent.

"No worries. I see you speak English," Lance replied as he couldn't help but admire the woman's natural beauty.

"Yes, I speak English. I studied in England for a couple of years and I learned to speak English fairly well. I wouldn't profess to be fluent, but I do well enough to understand and be understood", as she smiled at Lance.

"I'm Lance", as he extended his hand out to shake hers.

"I'm Garbella; please to meet you", as she shook his hand, made eye contact, and smiled.

"That is a unique name. What does it mean?"

"It means heavenly", as she smiled showing her pearly white teeth. "Are you American?" as she flashed those hazel eyes at Lance.

"Yes, I'm in Rome for business but I decided to take

advantage of the opportunity to do a little shopping. Milan has so many choices and I enjoy new sites", as he gently kissed her hand.

"You are such a gentleman."

"Do you live here in Milan?"

"No, I live in Rome. I'm here shopping as well. I wanted to get away from the tourism of Rome.

"Would you like to get a coffee?"

"Yes, I would like that very much", as the couple walked down the cobblestone street. There were many small cafes along the shopping corridor. They placed their orders and found a quiet table by the window.

"So do you visit Milan a lot for shopping or do you come here occasionally?"

"I enjoy getting away every once in a while. I like the quiet and laid-back pace here. I like to enjoy good coffee, drinks, and interesting conversations."

"What about our conversation?" as he sat back in his chair.

"Yes, you do. I think you are interesting, charming, and fun. You seem like you enjoy life to the fullest."

"I do enjoy life."

The couple continued to talk over the next couple of hours. They discussed everything from politics, to the environment. They connected on various levels.

"It's getting late. I have really enjoyed our conversation. It's amazing how fast time passes when you are having fun", as the two of them laughed.

"Do you have plans for dinner?" Lance casually asked.

"No, I was just going to dine alone or order room service."

"I was going to do the same since I'm unfamiliar with

Milan. Do you have any good recommendations? Would love if you joined me", as Lance made eye contact.

"I know a couple of places that are good. Where are you staying? We can get food near your hotel, or we can be more adventurous", she laughed.

The couple found a quaint little restaurant not far from where Lance was staying. The two decided to walk to the eatery. If they decide later to take a cab, it will be a short ride. They both enjoyed the exquisite and delectable food. The wine was locally grown. Lance and Garbella toasted one glass after another as they laughed and cherished the moment and ambience.

"I see you can drink", as Lance laughingly shook his head at Garbella.

"We are Italians and we believe in eating, drinking, and being merry. Right now, I want to be drinking", as she burst into laughter with Lance following shortly behind her.

The two finally left after finishing five bottles of wine. Garbella had finally reached her limit after drinking more than Lance.

"You just wanted to get me tipsy so you could take advantage of me", as she staggered a little upon getting up from her chair.

"No, that is not what I would do. I had a great time. You are a lot of fun", as he held her hand.

"You are sweet", as she leaned over to give him a gentle kiss on his neck.

"Thank you. You are sweet as well. You can catch a taxi back to your hotel from my hotel instead of the restaurant. I would feel more comfortable with you leaving from there", as the two walked back toward Lance's hotel.

"We were so close to your hotel. I didn't realize we were only a few blocks away. The air is refreshing."

"We are here. Would you like to come up for a minute? We can have some coffee or just talk," Lance casually said as he looked into Garbella's glazed eyes.

"I would like that", as the couple got on the elevator. Lance had a luxury suite with a balcony overlooking the courtyard. Garbella held Lance's hand on the elevator as she continued to make provocative eye contact. It was a short walk from the elevator to his suite. She put her arms around his waist as he pulled her close to his chest.

As soon as Lance walked through the door, Garbella rubbed over his chest as he pulled her close for their first kiss. Garbella leaned her head back to feel the reward of their lips touching. Lance tongue glided over hers, as he tasted her sweet lips. He had been thinking about those lips the entire night as he watched her talk and laugh.

Within seconds, Garbella started aggressively kissing him, as she took off his tie and ripping the buttons from his shirt. The passion was intense between the two of them. Lance and Garbella's intense, animalistic passion surfaced as his hands explored the contours of her womanly features. Garbella knew what she wanted and she felt Lance knew how to give it to her. Within seconds, she turned around, arched her back, leaning her head into Lance's chest. She aggressively placed his hands along the inside of her thighs as she breathed heavily. Lance raked his fingernails along the inside of her thigh, upward with her every deep but passionate breath as he licked the back of her neck. Finally, Garbella could no longer take the passionate tease. She showed her craving for Lance by turning around and licking his chest, his face, and sucking his fingers.

Garbella dropped to her knees as she gave Lance unfounded pleasure by licking the inside of his thigh grabbing his manhood with one hand and gripping Lance's ass with her other hand. She looked up at him as she gave him pleasure licking the tip of his cock with her tantalizing tongue. Lance leaned back as he grabbed her hair pushing her face down on his manly tool of pleasure until he could hear her gagging. Garbella stood up, licked Lance's chest, and bit his nipples.

Lance strong arms grabbed Garbella and placed her on the counter with her legs draped over his shoulders. He looked up at her with each upward lick as she grabbed a handful of his ebony mane. Her breathing got shorter and faster in anticipation of him tasting her. He slid her soaked panties to the side as he tasted her neatly trimmed treasure. Her pussy was throbbing as she mentally begged him to go deeper inside with his agile tongue. Finally, Lance gently opened her sodden lips and licked upward on her clit tasting her womanly nectar. Garbella entire body trembled with pulsating sensations as Lance sucked on her clit with his finger exploring her G-spot.

"Fuck", as Garbella's thighs clenched around Lance's head. She gasped as if he had stolen her last breath as she whimpered desperately trying to catch her breath.

He turned her around and bent her over the counter. Garbella arched her back as she grabbed the edge of the counter. Lance squeezed her nipples as he licked the back of her neck. Aggressively, he grabbed a handful of her long brown hair as he slid inside of her soaked lips. She moaned with pleasure breathing deeply. She panted as he went deep inside and then pulled out.

"I think it's wet now. Can you feel me inside." as he slid his hardness back inside. Lance bent her over the counter as he grabbed her shoulders pumping her harder and deeper with each thrust. He raised her dress exposing her round ass. Lance grabbed, squeezed, and slapped her ass as he went furiously in and out. Garbella's chest rose and fell as Lance drove inside her hard and fast. He took his fingers off her shoulders grabbing a handful of her brown hair while pushing her down on the counter. Her hands gripped the edge of the counter with each of his manly thrusts. Garbella arched her back and moaned loudly sounds of ecstasy. Lance bit the side her neck and sucked on her earlobes as Garbella turned around to give him intense kisses as he pumped her.

Moments later, Garbella slid her drenched panties off, un-snapped her bra, and got on her hands and knees on the oversized leather chair; grabbing the backrest. Lance slid inside of her, teasing her by pulling his hard cock in and out, as he rubbed the tip along her soaked lips. She gasped each time he went inside and pulled out.

"I need it now. Stop teasing me."

"What do you want?"

"Fuck me baby. Give it to me now. Pull my hair."

"You've been bad," Lance growled in a deep huskily voice.

"I've been bad," she whimpered in a high-pitched tone.

"Now I'm going to spank your ass!"

"Yes, please spank my ass", she uttered in a whimpering tone. Lance pumped her hard and fast; thrusting more vigorously with each motion.

Lance grabbed her by the hand and took her out on the balcony. Garbella held onto the balcony as Lance came up behind her. Lance slid his hands underneath her dress to feel her hardened nipples. Garbella leaned her head back as she turned slightly for their tongues to touch. She bent over the balcony as he entered her soft, wet sugar walls. Lance hips gyrated slowly as he explored all the contours of her inner treasure. Garbella covered her mouth to prevent from screaming the sounds of passion and ecstasy.

A passing security guard heard the whimpering and looked up to see where the sounds were coming from. The guard paused for a second, nodded his head, as he made eye contact with Lance before continuing his rounds. Moments later, the couple went back inside and retired to the bedroom to finish their animalistic sexual encounter.

The next morning, Garbella rolled over to feel Lance's presence. Lance was not in bed. He was sitting on the balcony.

"I ordered you some breakfast."

"Thanks", as she put on a robe and joined him overlooking the morning activities down in the courtyard.

"You were amazing last night", as he smiled at her.

"It was the wine," she quickly replied as her eyes rolled while she twirled her hair.

"Well, I will have to take some of that wine home with me", he jokingly replied.

"I have to get going."

"Well at least have breakfast with me."

"That sounds good."

The couple enjoyed breakfast and a relaxing conversation. Shortly afterwards, Garbella showered and departed for her trip back to Rome. She savored and re-lived the moments and memories as her body responded to the absence of Lance.

CHAPTER 9

MONICA called Vito to see how the meeting with Lance went. She had genuine concerns that if he didn't invest in the venture, Lance would fail and inevitably, her agency would miss out on an excellent and lucrative opportunity. In addition, Monica had emotional turmoil regarding Vito. After what had happened between them, she vowed she would never contact him again. This venture was the catalyst that reopened emotional wounds she thought she had gotten past. For now, she tried to focus primarily on the business.

"Vito Volsi office, how may I direct your call," the receptionist replied.

"I'm trying to reach Vito," Monica replied in a calm voice.

"Hold on one moment while I see if he is available."

"Hello, how are you? I didn't expect to hear from you", Vito spoke in his deep Italian rich accent.

"Hello, Vito. I wanted to call you to see how things went with Lance Howard. He came to see you about a business venture and I wanted to see how things went and if you considered investing", she spoke as she fought to hold her emotions back.

"I met with him. I turned him down. There were too many unknowns. Besides, I told you if you needed money, I would give you whatever you needed."

"I see you can give me money now but you couldn't give me what I wanted years ago. Some things never change," she sharply replied.

"We both knew the situation. I made mistakes. I'm living with the regret now and will be living with the regret and your resentment for the rest of my life. I guess some things weren't meant to be."

"Really, I can't believe you but I won't even continue this conversation. I'm hanging up."

"Wait, have dinner with me!"

"Vito, you are still married. What part of this whole situation that you don't understand?"

"Why? What is the point? Nothing has and will ever change."

"I'm at a different point. I only want to see you. Just have dinner with me; nothing more. I just want to lay eyes on you once again."

"Vito, what good will that do for either of us?"

"Let's not have this conversation on the phone. I will be in DC tomorrow. We can just talk," he pleadingly replied.

"I don't know. I don't think that is a good idea. You hurt me," she replied as the tears streamed down her cheeks.

"I realized that I hurt you and I was wrong. Let's just meet. That is all that I ask of you at this point. Will you do that for me?"

Monica hesitated for seconds what seemed like a lifetime for Vito. Finally, she made the decision to see Vito for lunch. In her mind, she needed closure and Vito wasn't going to go away. Monica needed the liberating strength to face this emotional hurdle. This was the turning point.

"We will have one last conversation in person after that, I can't see you anymore. It's too painful."

"Thank you. I will call you when I land and we can have lunch tomorrow and just talk."

"Yes, give me a call on my cell number", as she provided the number to him.

Vito called his personal assistant to tell him to have the jet ready for travel to Washington DC ASAP.

Monica did meet Vito. The two of them had an emotional late lunch. They discussed so many things: things that went wrong between the two of them and how neither of them was the same. Vito agreed to let Monica go emotionally. Monica finally found the strength she needed to move forward with her life as she left his hotel room.

* * *

[Phone Rang]

"Hello, this is Lance."

"Hey Lance. This is Jon. I wanted to give you quick call to see when you will be back in Chicago. I have another business associate that may be interested in your venture. Besides, we can catch up and see how things went in Brazil with Lucas."

"Well my schedule is tight right now. It looks like I won't be able to get back in town for a couple of weeks maybe three. I will contact your office to check your availability."

"Lance, that sounds good. Just let me know and I will communicate the scheduling information with my business associate. Until then, I will chat with you soon."

Lance had his suspicions about Jonathan. Was this the same man he met a few months ago? Jonathan was being very nice to Lance, which contradicted everything against his gut instinct that something wasn't right. The real question was what? [Perhaps I will look into Jonathan a little more closely to see if he has any "dirt" I needed to know. I will call my cousin Sammy in Chicago.]

[Garbella Phone Rang]

"Hello Garbella, how are you?"

"I'm doing well", as her eyes widened from the sound of Lance's voice as she twirled her hair.

"I just wanted to make sure you got back to Rome safely."

"Thank you so much for calling. I am still smiling from Milan", as she giggled and eyes rolled.

"You are most welcome."

"Do you ever visit Rome", she curiously inquired.

"Not on regular basis but I enjoyed the sites, the food, and the wine. I also enjoyed something else", as he hummed.

"Well if you ever come back to Rome, definitely let me know", as she exhaled and relived a brief moment on the balcony.

"I will definitely let you know."

Lance boarded the jet and headed to Chicago. He wanted to meet with his cousin Sammy. Lance's gut feeling was telling him that something just wasn't right with Jonathan. Given the initial exchange, there is another side. Besides, if he is interested in lining up all these investors but he isn't investing in the venture, there must be a reason.

The plane touched down in Chicago. Lance was a little tired from the long trip. However, he did sleep during some on the flight. Lance's driver picked him up from the airport and dropped him at his hotel.

"Sammy, I just landed."

"It's good to hear from you. I was surprised to receive your call. What's going on with you?"

"We can't discuss this over the phone. Can we meet tomorrow evening?"

"Sure! You can come by the restaurant. It will be good to see you. It's been years now."

"I know", as Lance hung up the phone.

[Candice: Hi, Lance. I hoped your trip to Brazil was good.]

[Lance: Yes, it was a good trip. I got a new investor onboard.]

[Candice: Wow! That is great. Will I ever see you again?]

[Lance: Definitely. Hopefully, things will slow down soon at least for a minute. I have lots of things to share with you.]

[Candice: That sounds great. I will let you get back to business. Call me sometimes]

Lance took a brief moment to evaluate all the people in his life. Candice is a sweetheart. She keeps in touch and is easy-going. We always have a good time. Unfortunately, I have so many things going on that I haven't had a chance to process much. Right now, I have to stay focused on the business.

[Phone Rang]

"Hello Lance. This is Monica Salazar.

"Hi Monica, what is going on," as he sat in his hotel room reviewing his notes.

"Did you think any more about the condos we saw when you were in DC?"

"Honestly, I haven't, but I was interested in the one in Potomac. I believe it was the last one."

"Yes, it was the last property we saw. What was the price on that one again?"

"The listing price is $1.2 million, but since the property has been on the market for a while, and it's slow for condo sales, I think we can offer $950,000 dollars."

"Let's go with that offer. You can fax me the paperwork to the number at the hotel", as he read her the number.

"I will send that information over shortly."

"Thanks."

"Do you have any prospects for a land purchase for the stadium?"

"Actually, I do. I'm working a lead on a commercial plot of land that may be an option. I will explore more and let you know."

"Thanks Monica. I will call you when the contract paperwork arrives to confirm I received the documents."

"I would appreciate you closing the loop."

"That is not a problem", as Lance ended the call.

Lance arrived at his cousin's restaurant mid to late afternoon before the dinner rush. Sammy and Lance spent a couple of summers together in New York. Although they didn't talk often, the two cousins maintained a closeness over the years.

"Sammy, it's good to see you. It's been way too long", as the two men hugged.

"I know. I see life has been treating you well. I see you

'put on' a few pounds but you still look good. What's going on with you?"

"Is there somewhere we can speak in private?"

"Sure, we can meet in my private office in the back. What is going on now? I'm getting worried."

"I have a real estate deal working for a soccer franchise and stadium. I have an issue: Jonathan Westin is connected to most of my investors or he introduced them to me. Although Jonathan is not personally invested in the joint venture, he is involved indirectly. My gut feeling tells me that something is not right with this guy. I need more information. However, Jonathan is wealthy and powerful. He also has a lot of connections so I have to be very careful."

"Cousin, you are so right. I have heard of Jonathan Westin. He is a very sadistically and dangerous man. I have heard stories of people that have disappeared when they crossed him for the most insignificant thing," Sammy replied as his eyes narrowed with a look of concern.

"Sammy, I need information. I need to know whom he talks to and what is being discussed. I don't really know how 'deep' this whole situation goes."

"Lance what you need is a wire on the inside and a clone program."

"A clone program, what does a clone program do," Lance replied with intrigue.

"A clone program allows you to clone the profile of a wireless device such as a phone or tablet. You only need to be within five feet of the device for 60 seconds to download the program. The program loads in the background and takes up virtually no memory. A person doesn't even need to touch the 'mark' device. All this occurs via Wi-Fi. Once loaded, the marked device will transmit everything in real time to include voice and text communication. The receiving station will hear and see the same information the marked device is sending or receiving.

"Wow, I didn't know this kind of technology existed", Lance replied in disbelief.

"Technically it doesn't. The government, under a special surveillance initiative, developed it but the program eventually found its way onto the 'black-market' to the highest bidder. There are only a few people in the country that knows about the program and even fewer people that knows how to write these kinds of programs."

"Sammy, do you know any of those people?"

"Yes, a friend of mine is one of those people, and he lives here in Chicago. His name is Pearson Caldwell."

"What! Isn't he the software developer for hospital administration programs to streamline operations?"

"Yes, but what a lot of people don't know is that Pearson used to be in the Army and that he worked in cyber and intelligence operations. He doesn't mention that fact and he keeps a very low profile by not discussing what he did in the Army.

"How long have you known him?"

"I have known him for years. He trusts me."

"Can you talk to him and set up a meeting. Don't tell him who we are targeting for information gathering," Lance hesitantly responded.

"Don't worry about that being an issue. He never wants to know whom you want to 'spy' on for whatever reason. He only writes the program."

"Sammy, I'm going to owe you big time", as he hugged his cousin.

"Lance no worries. We are family! I will set up the meeting. I will call you with the details in a couple of days."

Lance left the meeting with a newfound depth of insight. His thoughts were running uncontrollably about the information he had just learned. He went back to his hotel room and devised a plan to target Jon's phone and a few other key surprises. If Jon is an honest man and above board on this real estate deal, then all is well. Otherwise, Lance needed to know if his gut feeling was right.

A couple of days later, Sammy set up the meeting out on a chartered boat. Only the three men and a two-person boat crew were aboard. "Pearson Caldwell, this is Lance Howard, my cousin", as Lance extended his hand.

"I'm pleased to meet you", as Pearson shook his hand. "Sammy tells me you two spent summers together in NYC. He also tells me that you are his favorite cousin."

"Well, Sammy and I do go back a long ways. We kept in contact throughout the years. I have always been able to count on him and he could always count on me."

"It's good to have people you can trust," as Pearson looked Lance straight in the eye.

"I agree," as Lance maintained eye contact with Pearson.

"Pearson, I need your help. I need a clone program and a transmitter."

"It will cost $3 million dollar sent to this numbered account", as he pulled out his micro laptop for the transfer. Pay half now, and the other half when you get the device, transmitter, and the program. You will only need to be in the same room with the person for 60 seconds. The download is complete after 60 seconds. You will receive all communications from the targeted devices to your phone that I will provide to you. There will not be a need to meet again, and we will never discuss this meeting because it never happened," Pearson replied in a callous regimented tone.

Lance transferred the funds to the numbered account while on the boat. He would receive later instructions for the devices delivery and payment arrangements.

[Julie's Phone Rang]

"Hey Julie. How are you?"

"I'm great. I'm surprised you called", as she smiled.

"Yes, I am in town on business for a few days. Do you think you can pencil me in for a date?"

"I don't know. I will have my people contact your people", as she paused for a second before she burst into laughter.

"Saturday is a good day for me," she replied with coolness.

"You got me," Lance replied. "I see you really do have jokes."

"I will pick you up around 6:30pm on Saturday evening."

"That sounds good. I have a meeting. I will talk to you soon", as she ended the call.

The next day Lance received instructions to pick up his devices and wiring instructions. Everything was set for his upcoming meeting with Jon.

[Phone Rang]

"Lance, this is Monica."

"Hi Monica, how are you?"

"I'm great. I have great news! Our offer on the condo was accepted."

"That is excellent. We will have to celebrate when I get back to DC", as Lance laughed.

"We may be able to do that," she replied.

"I have a commercial property I want you to look at when you get back in town as well. The property has potential as a suitable site for the soccer stadium."

"That is fantastic", as Lance eyes widened with raised eyebrows.

"I will continue to research other sites as well. I should have those ready for you to look at when you return for the closing."

"That sounds good. Send me the details on the commercial property. I would like to at least look at some pictures."

"I will."

Lance received instructions on how and where to pick up his surveillance items and payment arrangement. He successfully picked them up and transferred the money. The only thing remaining now was to get in the room with Jon and set things in motion.

Saturday arrived, and it was date night with Julie. Julie seemed really nice, mysterious, and reserved. Lance wanted to get to know her. In his mind, Julie was a unique classy woman. Lance picked her up around 6:30 that evening. The couple anticipated the delectable food at *Cellini,* a renowned Chicago restaurant. Julie mentioned she wanted to go to an Italian restaurant. Lance was very receptive to that idea given the fact he was Sicilian. The two enjoyed a quiet evening in a relaxed ambience.

"So Julie, tell me more about yourself. What do you want to be when you grow up?" he playfully asked.

"I want to be an astronaut, a fireman, and a police offi-cer," Julie replied with an emotionless look on her face. Lance stared in disbelief as his eyes rolled.

"I'm only joking Lance. You really have to lighten up."

"I know. You got me once again. I see you like to laugh and enjoy life. All these are good things. Lance proposed a toast: To laughter and life." The two of them enjoyed their dinner and later went for a quiet stroll along the pier.

"Julie, I'm surprise you are single. You are warm, funny, caring woman and definitely beautiful. How long have you been divorced?"

"I have been divorced a little over three years. It's been a big adjustment for me. I went through a nasty divorce and custody battle. The whole thing has taken its toll on me emotionally."

"I'm sorry if I touched on a sore emotional subject. We can get back to our regularly scheduled program, if that is better," Lance replied as he grabbed her hands as he looked into her eyes. Julie's eyes fixated on Lance's as he pulled her close and gave her a kiss. He held her close as they both enjoyed the moment. He took her home shortly after their walk and kiss.

"Julie, I had a really nice time tonight."

"I enjoyed my time as well Lance. You are a gentleman", as she turned to open her door. "Let me know when you get back to your hotel."

"Sure, I will let you know."

[Julie sat down and enjoyed the thoughts of the quiet evening with Lance. It's been a long time since she had been on a date. She hadn't really dated since her and Pearson broke up. She questioned herself many times, about how things unfolded with her and him. She missed the fun things they used to do together. Lance reminded her of Pearson. She pondered if she should give him a call. It's been several months since they last spoke. In her mind, Julie couldn't get Pearson out of her thoughts. She often replayed the events in her mind about how she and Pearson fell apart. Julie decided to rekindle things with Pearson. She realized that after her date with Lance, she still had emotions for Pearson.]

[Pearson's Phone Rang]

"Hello Pearson, this is Julie Barber"

"Hello Julie, It's good to hear from you."

"I know it's been a long time. I have been through a lot lately. I have been meaning to call you but I just couldn't bring myself to call. I wasn't sure what I was going to say."

"There is no need to explain. We all go through things in life. I'm happy to hear from you."

"I am happy to hear your voice as well."

CHAPTER 10

[THREE Years Earlier]
Things were going well between Julie and Pearson. The dramatic events of the "blackmailing" letters were finally getting farther away from the current events in Julie's life. Up to this point, Julie held her secret closely. She could not risk the chance of Pearson finding out about how divisive and manipulative she had acted during all the events. In her mind, she had done nothing wrong.

Her divorce was in the process of being finalized with the final hearing scheduled in the upcoming weeks. Although her soon to be ex-husband had taken her through a significant emotional experience with the unreasonable demands and nasty custody battle, her heart was sadden knowing that within weeks, her marriage would be over. Ten years of her life that she shared with a man and had a child with would soon drastically change. Julie questioned her decisions and had deep remorse related to ending the marriage. Perhaps she was the person that caused the marriage to end. She thought, perhaps she didn't work hard enough to work things out. Julie's parents had been married over forty years. Her mom had three children, a career, and a marriage to a politician. There personal life was constantly being scrutinized, but her parents were able to make things work. What was her parent's secret and why did she fail after only ten years? Julie continued down this self-persecuting thought path.

In addition to the stigma surrounding her divorce, Julie was also dealing with the guilt of hiding the secret about the letters from Pearson. She still could not believe she had allowed herself to be in such a precarious situation in the first place. Why did she allow herself to be in such a compromising situation at work? This was her career, well-being, and a means to take care of her son. Julie could not believe she had been so irresponsible. She had compromised her moral values, her integrity, and had violated Pearson's trust. Although Julie questioned her actions, she had a disturbing perspective of "what Pearson doesn't know, won't hurt him." Besides, secretly, she enjoyed the attention. She often thought back to the days when she was in high school. Her overprotective brothers didn't allow much social interaction. Coupled with her father's high political profile, Julie didn't get a chance to lead a normal life. Her parents instilled in her early how she was supposed to act, speak, and behave. Neither she nor her brothers should behave in a way that would bring shame or embarrassment to the family. Although she loved her parents, she resented the fact that she had to consider the political implications first and foremost in all her actions. Hence, she had a rebellious motivation to attend college far away from the political pressures and influences associated with her father in Maine.

For now, Julie was in a very dark place emotionally. She felt isolated and devalued. She could not share the emotional turmoil with anyone because she had created this quandary and was solely responsible for her own actions regarding Pearson. Julie thought about how Pearson cared for her deeply and the only thing he ever wanted from her was for her to be honest with him. However, in her mind, she had betrayed that trust, and she really didn't know how to mend this offense.

Julie continued the rouge between her and Pearson. Although she never shared the details of the bed and breakfast get-away with anyone, secretly she enjoyed the attention and the uninhibited sexual expression. From a fantasy perspective, Julie was turned-on by the fact that she was being watched. As the daughter of a prominent senator, she never really had an opportunity to explore her sexuality. She had to be "politically correct" by getting married, having a couple of kids, and leading a normal uneventful life. However, unknowingly, in college Julie seized the opportunity to realize her lesbian fantasies. Although she only dated a couple of guys in college, Julie enjoyed exploring instances involving feminine touch. During an off campus party, she discovered a new and exciting element of her sexuality. She loved the traditional and protective aspects of being in a man's arms. However, there were times where she longed for the gentle touch of a woman. Although she preferred a predominately-heterosexual relationship, she occasionally ventured mentally to explicit and sensual encounters with a woman. Most of Julie's thoughts were fantasies perpetuated from reliving the exciting and adventurous girl-on-girl rendezvous from college.

Julie had buried her bi-sexual emotions as her life had taken a more traditional path. Although her marriage ended, she enjoyed the security associated with marriage especially the part involving being a mother. This was her opportunity to nurture her child by allowing him the freedom to be a child without the pressure and ramification associated being in the public 'spotlight.'

After the court hearing to finalize the divorce, Julie was overwhelmed with emotions. Julie called Pearson to let him know her divorce was final.

"Pearson, I know you are a wonderful man and you have been supportive throughout this entire daunting process. I don't mean to push you away, but I really need some time."

"Julie I know. You haven't been yourself leading up to the hearing. I know this is a significant emotional event. Although I haven't been married, I still remember when my parents divorced. It was an emotional and traumatic event for me. Take some time and give me a call when you are ready to talk."

"Thanks. I am glad you are in my life", as she ended the call.

Julie took some time to adjust to the fact that her life was different now. Although her ex-husband hadn't live in the house in over two years, she still struggled with the fact that now she was no longer married and was a single mother.

About a month after her divorce, Julie received a random phone call from a number she didn't recognize. The caller left a message:

[Hi Julie, this is Jennifer Sanders from Tinsel University. We went to college together. I know it's been years since we spoke. I heard you still lived in the Chicago area. Give me a call so we can catch up.]

Julie was overwhelm with excitement from the surprise phone call. She hadn't spoken to Jen since their years in undergrad. Jen was her first female lover. Hearing her voice after all, these years revived her imagination of their numerous encounters. Julie felt comfortable with Jen for so many reasons. She was at an emotional low point with the recent chaos and Jen's timing was perfect.

Julie called Jennifer back.

"Hi Jen, it's been way too long. How are you? How did you get my number? What's going with you these days?" Julie was full of excitement like a new college co-ed.

"Julie, I got your number from the school alumni directory. I picked up one and saw your name listed. I've been meaning to call you for months, but I just hadn't gotten around to doing it until now. As for me, I finished undergrad in psychology and eventually went to law school. I know, I didn't think I was attorney material either," as the two of them laughed.

"Jen, are you married? Do you have any kids?"

"No, Julie, I'm not married. I haven't had time to settle down and have a family. Hell, I will be lucky if I can keep a steady man. I focused on my career, and it has really paid off. What about you?"

"I was married, now recently divorced. I have a son (he is twelve). I'm still getting adjusted to being single again. I have this guy that I am seeing, but we are taking a mini break because I needed some time. That is enough about me, what brings you to town?"

"There is a lawyer's conference next week. I live in Seattle now, but I will be in town next week. I would love to catch up for dinner and just talk."

"That sounds great. I will look at my calendar, but it should be ok. I will work something out."

"That sounds great. I will give you a call when I arrive in town."

The following week, Julie and Jenifer met for dinner downtown. The two hadn't seen each other in years, but they reconnected as if no time had passed.

"Julie, it's so good to see you after all these years", as the two women embraced.

"I'm so glad you reached out. I know life can get hectic and time passes so quickly. You are still looking well. What is your secret?"

The two continued to catch up through small talk with food and drinks. Julie hasn't had a good time like this since before her divorce. She had been at a very low point emotionally for a while. The two ladies finished their dinner and headed to the hotel lounge. They got a table and enjoyed the piano playing as they continued drinking.

"Jennifer, you are still fun. I haven't drunk this much since college. You always knew how to bring out the adventurous side in me."

"Well Julie, I like to have a good time. Life is too short and you should 'burn the candle at both ends' and live life to the fullest."

"Jen, you are so right. I'm single again, and it's time to live life on the edge. However, I'm drunk right now so it will have to start tomorrow", as the two women burst into laughter.

"I had such a good time. I will have to catch a cab home. I'm way too drunk to drive.

"Julie you can crash at my hotel room. I have two queen beds. It's a nice suite. You know us lawyers; we are always negotiating for a better deal."

"You sure it's ok. I don't want to impose."

"Don't be silly. It's late, and we can have brunch unless you have to be somewhere early in the morning."

"No, I'm good. My son is with his dad this weekend."

"Well it's settled. Let's get out of here before the creepy old men show up and start hitting on us," as the two ladies laughed loudly and looked around to see if anyone noticed. Julie and Jen arrived at the hotel suite. The suite was exactly as Jen described. The room was spacious with a separate sitting area from the bedroom overlooking Lake Michigan.

"Julie do you want a glass of wine from the min-bar?"

"Sure, this room is very nice. Even at night, the view is amazing."

The ladies toasted, reconnected, and caught up on life. They both were looking out the window. Jen put her glass down and rubbing her hands on Julie's shoulder and along her neck gently massaging along the base of her neck. Julie leaned her neck back as she relaxed as Jen touched her.

"Your hands are wonderful. You must know I am stressed. With the divorce and work, I have been so overwhelmed."

"I can only imagine. There is no need to worry. I want you to relax and enjoy", as Jen continued rubbing her neck. Julie always felt comfortable around Jen. Tonight was no exception. Jen continued rubbing her shoulders, along her waist and up to her perfectly rounded breasts. Her hands cupped them gently exploring the contours of her womanly peaks. Julie let out a heavy sigh as she enjoyed the sensual touch. Jen turned her around and the two friends' lips touched as gently as a breaker reaching the ending on the beach before returning to the sea. Their tongues touched and teased each other as the sexual tension elevated. Jen caressed, licked, and explored all of Julie's erotic treasures as both women undressed to feel the sensation of each other's' skin. Jen continued as she licked the inside of Julie's thigh, sucked her fingers, and swirled her tongue around the tips of her nipples. Julie breathing became shorter and deeper as her anticipation intensified. Finally, Jen's tongue found its way along the inside of Julie's thigh up to her wet pond of passion. Julie was throbbing at this point. Jen's gentle tongue traced the contours of Julie womanly lips. Julie moaned huskily as she arched her back. Jen fingers explored Julie's G-spot as her tongue flickered up and down on her clit. Julie could no longer take the stimulation and exploded with ecstasy creating a flood of womanly juices down her thighs. Jen licked her gently quenching her passionate thirst.

The two women slipped into slumber cuddling and spooning in the same bed. Each woman satisfied from the rekindling of passionate emotions from the past. Both sexually satisfied on multiple levels.

The next morning both ladies enjoyed a delicious brunch courtesy of hotel room service. Each laughed about how drunk they were and how the evening ended with a magical climatic conclusion. Julie got dressed and kissed Jen just before she departed.

"I had a really good time. Will I see you again Jen?"

"Do you want to see me again?"

"Yes, I would like that a lot", as she made eye contact looking deeply into Jen's eyes.

"I would like to see you again as well. I can fly back and we can spend the weekend together."

"I would like that a lot."

"I will call you when I get back to Seattle."

"That sounds great", as she waved upon leaving the hotel room.

They vowed to stay in touch by calling/texting each other on a regular basis. Julie enjoyed the excitement of something new. The new relationship took her mind away from the hurt and disappointment associated with her recent divorce. Because of Julie's tight schedule, Jen did fly back to Chicago a few times and the two of them enjoyed wonderful weekends.

Pearson noticed that Julie called him less and less. He could sense something was going on but couldn't quite put 'his finger on it.' Julie was behaving differently; distance, less responsive to his calls. She even cancelled a date. This was something she had never done in the past.

Finally, Pearson confronted her.

"Julie, what is going on with us these days?"

"I'm sorry, I have been going through a lot lately. I have so much on my mind. I'm trying to adjust to the fact that I am single again. I thought I would be married for life and that didn't work out. I'm a single mother and all of this is overwhelming. I like you a lot but maybe it's too soon to be dating at this point. I just don't know."

I understand Julie. I know you are dealing with a lot these days. It's never easy to end a relationship and given the fact that it was your marriage, I know that can be devastating. What do you want Julie?"

"I'm just not ready at this point to be in a relationship. Would you consider being friends?"

"Well that is not what I wanted and I see you as far more than just a friend, but I'm also realistic as well. I don't want to force you into anything. We can take a step back. If we are meant to be together, we will be together. As for now, we are friends."

"Thank you for understanding. You don't know how much this means to me. You are a good man", as Julie turned away. She couldn't face him. She also couldn't tell him that she had been secretly seeing her girlfriend from college and that they had been sharing intimate rendezvous. These intimate encounters may have destroyed any chances of her and Pearson getting back together. For now, this was her life and she was enjoying the moment.

CHAPTER 11

L ANCE flew back to San Jose to check on the status of the upcoming software project. It was schedule to be release in the coming weeks. He had been in contact with his executive team to gauge the status of the project on a weekly basis. Things were coming along and the market had above average expectations for the new product release. If the project was successful, the software would propel Lance's company to the head of the pack with video sharing software.

The board had their monthly meeting to discuss the status of the business and upcoming project. Lance usually didn't attend every meeting, but since he was in town, he decided to attend. The board discussed new business, earnings reports, additional financials, and upcoming projects. It was a typical board meeting. After the meeting, Lance decided to head out and work from home.

[Phone Rang]

"Hello Lance. This is Vito. We met a few weeks ago. Did I catch you at a bad time?"

"No, I am just working. How may I help you?"

"I wanted to give you a call personally to let you know that I have reconsidered your proposal. I had my executive team review the financials. When will you be available to discuss the proposal in person?"

"I will check my calendar, but I should have availability on Monday. Will that work for your schedule?"

"Yes, I have availability all next week so Monday or Tuesday is fine."

"I will plan for Wednesday."

"That is fine. By the way, you can stay at the house when you arrive. I have plenty of room", as he laughed.

"I wouldn't want to impose."

"No, you wouldn't do that at all. I have over 12 bedroom suites. I'm sure my house staff can find room for you", as he chuckled.

"That sounds great. I will see you next week."

[Jon Phone Rang]

'Hello, this is Jonathan."

"The thing we discussed is happening in the next few weeks. I will let you know when I know more details."

"Thanks. I will call you later."

"Will I see you soon?"

"Yes you will see me soon."

Jon began his sinister plan to purchase all of Lance's company outstanding stock through a series of "shell" companies from around the world. Jon called the financial executives and began implementing his plan.

Lance arrived at Jonathan's office on Monday to meet with him to give him and update and obtain a lead on another prospective investor. Jon was even more cordial than the last time he saw Lance. On the surface, it would appear that Jon was genuinely trying to help Lance and his effort but that couldn't be farther from the truth.

"Hi Lance, it's good to see you again," as he shook his hand, smiled and patted him on the back. Lance smiled back.

"How are things going? How is the software business as well as the soccer venture going these days", Jon casually inquired.

"It's coming along well so far. I'm still working contacts and options for investors. I may have a prospective commercial lot for the stadium. I will head back to DC soon to explore the option."

"That sounds good. Looks like you have things moving forward. How did the meeting in Brazil go with Lucas?"

The meeting went well. He is onboard. I have a gift for you. Here is a handmade cigar lighter. I know how much you enjoy your Cuban cigars" as he reached over to hand the lighter to Jon.

"Thanks for the gift".

"Everything was great. Lucas 'put me up' at the estate. I met his family. His wife is an excellent cook. I could really get used to being in Brazil. By the way, Lucas has a beautiful daughter, Amelia" as Lance smiled.

"I can imagine. The last time I saw her she was 19 or 20 I believe. She was an attractive young lady then. I'm sure her beauty will continue to flourish."

"I like the women here in Chicago. They are a lot different from the ones in Cali. I recently went on a date with a classy woman I met here in Chicago."

"Oh really, what is her name and what does she do here in Chi-town," Jon casually inquired.

"Her name is Julie Barber, and she is a hospital administrator at one of the local hospitals. I can't remember which one," Lance replied with masculine enthusiasm.

Jon did not share his same enthusiasm. Jon eyes narrowed, mouth clenched, and hands sweated. His whole demeanor changed. He could not believe his ears. How dare Lance even mention Julie's name in relation to anyone other than himself. Jon continued to nod as Lance recounted some of the aspects of his date with Julie. The more Jon heard, the angrier he became. Jon was outraged and extremely infuriated.

"Well Jon, I wanted to drop by and give you an update. If anything drastically changes, I will give you a call. It was good to see you again."

"Lance, it was good to see you as well", as he gave him a half smile. The moment Jon thought Lance was out of the building, he began making calls to all of his business associates connected to this soccer venture.

Lance casually walked out of the building and his driver picked him up as scheduled. Once in the car, Lance looked at the PDA Pearson had modified for surveillance. The program was operating as designed. The PDA was capturing all communications both in texts and in phone calls. The surveillance device also downloaded the transcript to a designated server.

[Garbella's Phone Rang]

"Garbella, how are you?"

"I'm great. How are you doing? I'm surprised you called."

"Yes, I wanted to give you a quick call to let you know I will be in Rome tomorrow."

"Really?"

"Yes, I have some business in Rome, so I wanted to give you a call and see if you can squeeze me into your busy schedule?"

"Yes, of course", she replied with giddy excitement.

"I will give you a call when I land."

"I'm looking forward to seeing you. I thought I would never see you again. I just knew you were not coming back to Italy any time soon."

"Well things do happen", as he laughed. "I have to catch a flight. I will talk to you soon."

"Ciao!"

Lance boarded his jet in route to Rome. It was a long flight, but the time allowed him an opportunity to review material regarding the commercial property, relax, and get some much-needed rest.

Monica continued conducting the due diligence for the commercial plot of land. After extensive research and the evaluation of other properties, the 97 acres located North of Gaithersburg proved to be ideal for a soccer stadium. Now, it was only a matter of being able to negotiate a good price. The listing price for the property was $73 million. A firm out of Canada owned the property, which they purchased fifteen years ago. Monica was surprised that this large plot of land actually came on the market. Her firm began communications with the listing broker to determine the terms of the sale.

Lance's flight landed shortly after 11pm local time. The driver dropped him at his hotel. Lance couldn't wait to get settled and relaxed. It was a long flight and jet lag was quickly catching up with him. He texted Garbella from the plane to let her know he was a couple hours away from landing and that he felt it would be too late to call upon his arrival. Lance quickly took a shower and settled into bed.

The next morning, Lance alarm clock went off but

instead of his normal working out routine, he decided to take the morning off and sleep.

[Phone Rang]

"Hello!"

"Good morning sleepy head!"

"Hello, how are you? I wasn't sleeping."

"I'm glad you made it in safely. How was your flight?"

"It was good. I relaxed most of the way. I did get in some reading but overall, I rested."

"Good for you. Have you had breakfast yet?"

"Not yet. I will probably just order room service."

"Would you like me to bring you a cappuccino? Italy has the best cappuccino in the world."

"Yes, that would be nice. Where are you staying?"

"I'm at the Da Vinci Suites off of Plaza Circle."

"I know where that is. I should be there in about 30 minutes or so."

[30 minutes later]

"I'm here, what room are you in?"

"I'm in Room 341."

Minutes later, Garbella arrived at his door. Today she was wearing a sundress with sandals that showed her thin waist but curvaceous hips. Lance had on shorts, no shirt showing his hairy chest. He gave her a warm embrace upon her entry as he kissed her on the cheek.

"I see you made it here with no problems."

"Yes, you forgot. I'm from Rome", as she licked her tongue out at him.

"What was that for?"

"I'm being playful", as she smirked, then smiled.

"You will be punished", as Lance licked his lips." What did you bring me?"

"I brought the cappuccino as promised", as her eyes widened.

Lance order room service and the two of them enjoyed brunch and a relaxing conversation. The two of them melted into the softness of the comforter. Lance pulled her close to kiss Garbella's tender lips. He could feel her heat and passion.

"I missed you so much and so did my body," she whispered in his ear. She leaned her head to the side as Lance gently kissed the side of her neck. Lance nibbled on her earlobes and he breathed in her ear. Garbella breathing got shorter as she melted from Lance's mere touch.

Lance caressed and squeezed Garbella's body, kissing all over her as she leaned back in pure pleasure. He swirling his hot wet tongue on her nipples one by one, as she grabbed his head as her breathing shortened the faster he licked. Lance licked the back of her knees; along inside of her thighs; and the edge of her furnace. He asked her—"Do you want me to stop?"

"No", she uttered in a weak, whispering voice.

Garbella was on fire. Lance enjoyed teasing her. His tongue found its way to her special spot. Her pink love cave was neatly trimmed-throbbing in anticipation of his lip's first kiss. One gentle kiss led to another as he watched her every reaction. She flinched with each upward lick. His tongue traced the edges of her hotness with his tongue teasing her wet spot with each touch. She grabbed his head, arched her back, and clenched her legs uncontrollably the deeper his tongue went and the more his finger rubbed over her G-spot. Her erotic cream began to flow as she lost control in anticipation. Her whole body pulsated and gyrated with each soft lick of his tongue until her juices exploded opening up the floodgates of desire. Garbella almost passed out for a few seconds from the intensity of her eruption. He held and cuddled her until she recovered from the climatic rollercoaster.

Lance continued to please Garbella as no man had ever done. Their first lovemaking encounter was intense and animalistic. However, this episode was sensual, warm, and tender. Lance gave Garbella all the things she needed and none of the things she got at home. The two curled up on the sofa as they looked out the window.

"Lance, I could get used to this treatment", as she snuggled up next to him to feel his closeness.

"Yes, I see it didn't take you long to get here," he playfully replied as he rubbed her nose.

"The day has gone by so quickly. I know you have business to take care of; I just wanted to see you for a little while", as she kissed him before heading to take a shower. Garbella showered, dressed, kissed Lance, and departed on her way almost as quickly as she had arrived.

Lance reviewed the information regarding the commercial property. If this was the site, he wanted a better understanding of the various terms of the deal. Based on Monica's recommendation, this land project may be just the beginning of a wonderful business relationship. Only time will tell.

The next day, Lance checked out of his hotel and took a taxi to Vito's estate. Vito's house was a little over a 30-minutes' drive from Rome. Lance enjoyed the open clean air as he headed out into the bucolic landscape. The countryside reminded him of San Jose. The house staff greeted him and took his bags to his suite. The staff informed him that he was meeting Vito in the family room. Lance grabbed his laptop in case he needed to refer to financial information.

"Lance, it's good to see you again", as Vito extended his hand and patted him on the back.

"It's good to be back, although I was surprised by your call."

"Yes, sometimes in business an opportunity is not always obvious. Besides, I love soccer. I had my reservations because this business venture is outside of my normal industry. My family has been in the spirits business for almost 100 years. Although I have diversified into some other business areas, I primarily stick to what I know."

"I do understand."

"Look Lance, I'm interested in investing in your venture. You have heart, will, and passion. I see you steering this thing to fruition. I can just tell. I invited you here so I could get a chance to learn a little bit more about you."

"Thank you Vito. I know what I want and I go after it when I believe in something."

"Here is a letter of intent and my commitment to the venture for $150 million for a 30 percent financial interest."

Lance could not believe his eyes. What seemed like a lost cause turned out to be a blessing in disguise. He had finally raised enough funding to support his venture. He could obtain financing for the remaining expenditures.

"Hey Lance, are you working with any venture capitalists for this deal or are you working this deal on your own?"

"Vito, it's odd that you asked. I am in communication with Jonathan Westin. Jonathan isn't invested in the venture, but he has introduced me to some prospective investors. I'm championing the deal on my own," Lance delicately replied.

"Well I will tell you as one Italian to another: watch your ass with him. He is tricky, manipulative, and well connected. If he fell off the face of the earth, I wouldn't shed a tear for him", as his eyes narrowed and demeanor changed. "Enough about that prick, Let me show you around the place", as he led Lance from wing to wing.

As he entered the kitchen, his wife was preparing herself a snack.

"Lance let me introduce you to my wife, Garbella Li Volsi."

In shock, Garbella dropped the knife she was holding when she saw Lance's face in her house. Her eyes narrowed, tensed, as she took a deep breathe fighting to maintain her composure. Lance eyes widened as he too was in shock. He had no idea Garbella was a married woman. He never asked her, and she conveniently failed to mention that fact. However, they both were in a situation that could easily get out of control quickly.

Extremely irritated, Lance put forth his most poised posture as he extended his hand. "It's a pleasure to meet you Ms. Li Volsi", as Lance made brief eye contact, nodded and looked away.

"Call me Garbella. I'm not that old", she casually replied and smiled in an attempt to mask her true emotions.

"Well I'm going to let you men continue your business discussion or tour," as she quickly excused herself from the situation. She hurriedly headed to her master bath and locked the door. She held onto the sink as she faced herself in the mirror.

[I can't believe of all the business people in Italy that my lover happened to be doing business with my cheating fucking husband. He doesn't love me, but he keeps up this rouge as if I don't know. He is in love with Monica. I have known this for a very long time. Who cares who I'm doing! I know he doesn't. This is ironic payback for hurting me all those years. I'm his second wife as she exhaled, wiped her eyes, and fixed her makeup.]

"Vito you have a nice estate. The landscaping is marvelous. It reminds me of San Jose."

"Thank you. The gardeners do all the work. They keep the grounds looking amazing."

"They do a good job. Vito, I would love to continue our tour. However, the flight from California is weighing on me now. I would like to reconvene our tour a little later if you don't mind."

"Lance, I don't have a problem. I do understand. Jet lag is something that creeps upon you. Get some rest and we can talk later."

"Thanks", as Lance headed to his suite. He checked his phone and discovered he had five text messages from Garbella.

[Garbella: We need to talk] was the last message.

[Lance: call me. I am in my suite.]

"Lance, I will be at your door in 5 minutes." Moments later, she was at Lance's door.

Garbella exercised caution before entering Lance's suite.

"What the fuck," Lance furiously replied as he finally expressed his irritation.

"I can explain", Garbella exhaled.

"No, you never asked me if I was married."

"I see you conveniently left that part out."

"Keep your voice down."

"Why because you don't want your husband to hear us," Lance quickly retorted.

"No and if you have business with him, you can kiss that deal goodbye."

Lance lowered his voice. "You could have told me."

"You are right. I should have told you. I apologize", as she was overcome with emotions. Tears streamed down her cheeks.

"You have to stop crying", as he held her close.

"I know. Otherwise, my husband will figure this all out."

"I have to leave. I can't stay here. I will make up an excuse requiring me to head back to the US tonight."

"I understand", as she looked into his eyes. Lance kissed her.

"We can't see each other anymore. It's too risky. You better leave before someone accidently sees you come out of my room."

Garbella rubbed Lance's face, gave him one last kiss, and quickly departed his room undetected.

Later that evening, Lance met with Vito.

"Vito, I have to leave. I have an emergency at my company. I have a major project ongoing and there was a serious incident. I hope you understand."

"Lance, these things happen. Give me a call when you get back to the states and we can finalize any last requirements."

"Thank you for understanding", as Lance got into the car heading to the airport.

CHAPTER 12

LANCE headed to Washington DC. The closing date for the condo was coming up soon. He decided to use the extra time to meet with Monica and look at prospects for the stadium site. With the condo closing scheduled in a week, Lance could settle on the condo and move there instead of staying at a hotel. Having a residence would also give him an opportunity to begin socializing his ideas for a soccer stadium in the DC area.

"Monica, I just landed. How are things with you?"

"Things are going well. I have good news. I'm glad you were able to make it in safely. First order of business is the closing coming up next week. I can provide you the title company for wiring instructions for the funds."

"That sounds good. What else do you have on the agenda since I am in town?"

"I will get on Charles Franklin's calendar. He is the Senator for Maryland. We will need his support for the stadium initiative."

"I see you have been busy since I saw you last. I appreciate your efforts."

"Thank you. I get things done," she sarcastically replied.

"I see."

"Let me see if I can call his office and get on his calendar this week. I know it may be a long shot, but I will give it a try", as she excused herself to make a few calls. Several minutes later, she had secured an appointment two days from today.

"I see you have a lot of influence in this town", as Lance eyebrow raised.

"I do what I must", as she flung her head, checked her nails, and looked away.

"You are too much. By the way, how did the home inspection turn out?"

"There were no major issues. The inspector found a few things, but the seller will repair those items before next week's closing."

Lance headed to his hotel room. He had a lot of catching up to do. He hadn't had a chance to listen to the transcripts of Jon's conversations. There hadn't been any relevant information regarding the real estate deal that he knew of. On the surface, it looked like Jonathan actually was legitimately trying to get investors lined up to support Lance's venture.

[Phone Rang]

"Hello."

"Why are you calling me Garbella," Lance agitatedly replied.

"I didn't want you to leave angry. I admit that I was wrong for not telling you I am married. I didn't want to take the chance of you judging me and thinking less of me."

"Ok."

"Is that all you can say?"

"What do you expect me to say in this situation? Besides, I'm in business with your husband. I'm not going to do anything that would knowingly jeopardize our new business relationship. I'm sorry."

"I understand. I really enjoyed your company. You treated me special. I really enjoyed laughing and feeling wanted. I haven't experienced that feeling in a long time," she sadly replied.

"I enjoyed our time as well. I have to go. I will talk to you another time."

"Take care Lance", as she hung up the phone with tears streaming down her cheeks.

Two days later Lance, Monica, and Senator Franklin met in his office. Lance rode with Monica to the senator's office.

"To make sure you don't get 'blindsided,' today you will be meeting with Senator Franklin. He is an old politician that has been in the 'game' for a very long time. He understands how things get done. However, he is up for re-election in less than two years so he will be looking for 'campaign donations' to help him see how the stadium project will benefit the state. He is a very powerful and influential ally. He can either hurt or help your efforts. My suggestion is that you want him on your side."

"Thanks for the insight. I understand."

"Monica it's always a pleasant surprise to see you again. You are still getting younger like I imagined", as the Senator rose from his chair, eye widened as he cracked a devilish grin.

"Lance, let me introduce you to Senator Charles Franklin," Monica politely remarked.

"Please to meet you Senator", as he shook his hand.

"Have a seat. Can I offer you anything to drink, water, coffee, liquor?"

"No Senator, I'm fine," Lance politely responded. "Monica tells me you are coming up for re-election in the next couple of years. Well, as a new property owner in Maryland, I think it is important to have an effective political leader representing the State and initiatives that benefit the state. I fully support a person that has fairly and consistently represented the State all these years."

"Hell, Monica you didn't tell me you were introducing me to someone that bullshits almost as good as me. Notice I did say almost", as he leaned back in his chair, interlocking his fingers behind his head and chuckled. Monica laughed, and Lance awkwardly laughed as well.

"Now that we have that out of the way, let's get down to business", as he sat forward in his chair.

"Well, I'm proposing a stadium in Montgomery County. I'm looking for your legislative support, influence, and tax incentives for the first five years. In return, I will contribute to your re-election campaign and we all benefit", as Lance crossed his legs, while looking the senator in the eye.

"Monica, I like this guy already. I tell you what, if you find a way to share some of those big dollars you wealthy guys will be making from your soccer stadium in my state, I will make sure there is a soccer stadium in Montgomery County", he laughed as he lit up a Cuban cigar blowing smoke into the air.

"I'm confident I can persuade my business partners to agree", Lance laughed as he extended to shake the Senator's hand. The Senator leaned over and shook his hand with his cigar between his teeth.

"Monica, you are the best as always. Let me know what I can do for you. Unfortunately ladies and gentleman, I have another meeting," as he politely stood up to bid farewell to Monica and Lance.

"Monica, that didn't go as I expected, but overall I guess it turned out well."

"Lance, welcome to DC. That is how things get done in this town." Monica dropped Lance off at his hotel. Lance was busy with the upcoming product line scheduled for release. He reviewed the press release and other marketing materials for clarity and messaging. Since closing wasn't until next week, he used this time to listen to some of Jon's communication.

[Phone Rang]

"Hey Lance. Have you conquered the world yet", as she laughed.

"I see you have more jokes as always."

"Yes, you crossed my mind and I wanted to give you a quick call. I'm sure you are busy."

"Actually you have good timing. I have a lull in my hectic schedule. How is my favorite and sexiest flight attendant?"

"I'm doing well. I'm in Dallas. I have a long layover so I decided to give you a quick call."

"Thank you so much. When you get to your next destination, give me a call. I know we haven't spoken in a while."

"I will. Talk to you soon."

The following week, Lance's condo deal closed. Monica was busy setting up meetings to view the commercial lot as a possible site for the stadium. After coordinating with the listing agent, she confirmed an appointment.

"Lance, we are heading to look at the commercial property. Based on my research, I believe this is the most suitable option for the stadium. There were two other sites but the zoning restrictions would take too much time to overcome", as they drove to the location.

As the two of them walked around the entrance to the property, Lance inquired about some specific concerns.

"Monica, I have a few questions. Do we have engineering reports that I can review? Are there any environmental concerns for this site? I don't want to purchase a property and then find out the location is an environmental disaster. I know in California, environmental issues are deal breakers."

"Lance, I understand your concern. I took the liberty to have two different engineering firms conduct soil sample testing and geological evaluations. This venture represents a lot for both of us."

"I have the engineering reports, consultants involved, and other related professionals involved in making sure the due diligence is thoroughly conducted."

"What do you think of this location", as he looked Monica directly in the eye.

"This site is the best possible location in the DC area given the land and zoning restrictions. I think we should move forward and put an offer on this property. I do feel that 97 acres in the DC area will not last long on the open market."

"You may have a point." Land in the DC area is hard to come by especially a large plot of developable land. Lance decided to take Monica advice. He trusted her professional judgment. Lance submitted an offer of $60 million with a $5 million dollar down payment. He expected some negotiation from the seller. This offer would at least get the conversation started.

Lance returned to his hotel suite. Next week he would be in his newly purchased condo in Potomac, Maryland.

He had established a presence like Thomas Kent had rec-ommended. Things were lining up professionally toward getting his land venture underway. Lance had successfully raised $430 million dollars from letters of commitments from various investors. As he reviewed his company's stock, he noticed the upward trend. Lance believed the expected release of his new product was driving the upward stock price trend. Wall Street had a positive outlook with a strong buy rating. Overall, his portfolio was doing well. He sold several different stocks in order to fund the down payment and a large portion of the inevitably purchase price for the commercial property.

With all the funding in place and a strong possibility of securing the commercial land, Lance's hard work had finally paid off and his venture was showing life. He would soon be heading back to San Jose for the release of the new product line in the next few weeks. He expected to gain at least 17 percent of the video sharing social media market. His execu-tive team forecasted a 43 percent increase in market share and a 53 percent increase in stock price within the next quarter. Even if the projections were only half-right, Lance's company stood to gain a significant amount of money.

[Jon's Phone Rang]

"Jon, how are things treating you in Chicago? I should be back that way by the end of next week. I will fill you in on the details but I have secured the investors that I needed to make the deal work, and I have a solid offer on a commercial property in the DC area. It seems like things are looking up for this land venture," Lance enthusiastically reported.

"Wow that is excellent. You will have to come here so we can celebrate. I will call Lucas if you haven't already called him.

"No, I haven't called him yet. I just put the offer in on the property."

"Excellent! We will talk more when you get here. I have to run. Give me a call when you get into town."

"I will", as Lance ended the call.

[Candice Phone Rang]

"Hello Lance. What's up?"

"I just sealed a deal on my last investor, my company's stock is doing very well, and I have a contract on a piece of commercial property for my soccer stadium. I would say I'm doing pretty damn well; wouldn't you say?"

"Hell yeah! Sounds like you are doing exceptionally well."

"We will have to celebrate and get away. I know I have been promising to take some time off. Now I can finally breathe a sigh of relief."

"Are you in California?"

"No, I'm in DC wrapping up some business and then I will be heading to Chicago before returning to San Jose."

"What about you?"

"I'm in Dallas. Tomorrow, I am heading to Seattle. Let me know when you will be back in San Jose. We will have to really celebrate", as Candice took a deep breath.

"I'm looking forward to seeing you," Lance excitingly replied.

"I'm looking forward to seeing you as well. I have to go; it's time to board my flight", as Candice ended the call.

Finally, his condo was ready for occupancy. Lance decided to stay in DC in case he needed to be present for negotiations or to sign original documents. After a couple of weeks of intense negotiations, the two agencies reached a contractual agreement on the ninety-seven acres for $67 million dollars.

"Monica, this calls for a celebration."

"I agree", as she finally relaxed around Lance. "I will even pay for dinner."

"How nice of you," Lance retorted in a facetious tone.

Monica took Lance to *The Branch*, an exclusive restaurant on the southern border between Bethesda and Potomac. The secluded but quaint culinary jewel tucked away from the mainstream public only accepted reservations. Monica ordered wine for the both of them. Lance was impressed. As always, Monica continued to display her sophistication. Lance saw this as a unique turn-on the more he shared her presence.

"A toast: To long lasting business relationships," Monica proposed as she raised her glass. Lance joined her. The two enjoyed their dinner and a relaxing conversation. As promised, Monica did pick up the check for dinner.

"Thank you for dinner."

"You are welcome."

Monica arrived at Lance's condo building.

"I really enjoyed our dinner. Would you like to come up for coffee?"

"No, I will take a raincheck. I will take you up on that offer but not tonight," she replied.

"I do understand", as he slightly leaned forward to kiss her. Monica covered Lance's lips with her fingers.

"I can't Lance. You are a wonderful man. However, for personal reasons, I can't get personally involved with you. I'm sorry; I hope you understand."

Lance, stunned, leaned back, and looked away. "I

understand. I apologize for my actions", as he paused. "I'm going to go. I had a wonderful time", as he exited the car. Monica watched him enter the building and then drove away.

Lance poured himself a scotch, sat in the chair, and gazed out the window into the darkness. After finishing his drink, he took a shower and retired for the evening.

The next morning Lance completed his normal workout routine before starting his workday. As Lance was listening to the transcripts from Jonathan's communication, he made a disturbing discovery.

[Conference Call]

Jon: "Lucas, and Sabastian are you both on the line? If so, we will get started. I heard from Lance yesterday and he confirmed that he has successfully secured investment funding for the soccer franchise joint venture. With that said, we will soon have control over his financial interest. If not, he will otherwise suffer financial ruin. My plan worked just as I thought it would. Why would you doubt me? Did you not have faith that I couldn't 'pull' this deal off? I am Jonathan Westin and I always get what I want."

Lucas: "I know Jon. I have known you for years. I still can't believe he fell for this legerdemain; he is young though", Lucas laughed.

Sabastian: "Did you like how I started the whole thing?"

Jon: "We fed on him like easy prey in the jungle", as all three men laughed.

Jon: "Sabastian, I will be flying out to LA in about a week after I give that young protégé my ultimatum. I wish I could film his reactions, but I guess you will have trust my recount of the situation", as he chuckled.

Lucas: "Everyone is invited to join me at my estate. We

can formally celebrate while Lance Howard is 'licking his wounds' from the fallout."

Jon: "Thank you Lucas. We will see you in about a week."

Furious, Lance chartered a flight to Chicago to meet with Jonathan to confirm what he had heard on the transcript. He called Jonathan from the plane.

"Jon, I will be flying through Chicago in a couple of days instead of directly back to California. I decided to drop by and give you an update."

"That works. I will see you in a couple of days."

Lance flight landed in Chicago and he called his cousin Sammy to arrange an emergency meeting.

"Lance, what is going on", as his voice crackled with concern.

"I will fill you in when I see you." Thirty minutes later, Lance was at his cousin's restaurant.

"My gut feeling about Jonathan was right. He is a dirty snake. I don't know all the details, but I believe he plans to ruin me financially if I don't turn over my financial interest in this land deal."

"Oh Hell No! I'm from Chi-town, you fuck with my family; you fuck with me," Sammy viciously replied.

"I will let you know when I find out more details."

"Just say the word and I can take care of that son of a bitch and make it look like an accident."

"Hold on for now. I'm scheduled to meet with him in a couple of days. I should know more after the meeting. I will give you a call."

"Cousin, that's not a problem. You just say the word", as he was fuming and pacing the floor.

Two days later, Lance met Jon at his office. The two men exchanged pleasantries and quickly got down to business.

"Lance, I noticed your stock price is rising. Do you have a new product line scheduled to come online soon?"

"Yes, we have a new product line scheduled to be released soon. Why do you ask?"

"I asked because I know you value your company. You built it from 'scratch' so I do know you are passionate about your company.

"However, the reason you may not know why your stock price is soaring is because I own eighty-two percent of your company's outstanding shares. I have purchased almost all of the outstanding shares."

Lance, you have two choices: You can sell me your interest in this land venture, or I can "dump" all your company's stocks and drive your stock price down to nothing in a huge sell-off."

"What the fuck", as Lance angrily reacted. "This is 'blackmail."

"I thought you may be slightly upset", as Jon sat back in his chair behind his desk.

"Lance, you have 72 hours to decide. Is it going to be the land deal or your company? If I don't hear from you in the next 72 hours, I'm 'dumping' all your company's stock in the biggest sell-off in your company's brief history. Now, get the fuck out of my office."

Lance left Jon's office outraged and furious. He didn't want to call his cousin. He already knew what his cousin would do. However, he did call his cousin to give him an update.

"Sammy, that thing we talked about is worse than I

thought", as he hesitated to given him an update. Don't do anything until you hear from me."

"Just say the 'word' cousin; just say the 'word'", as he hung up the phone with Lance.

Lance called Candice. "Candice, where are you?"

"I'm in Phoenix. Lance what's the matter?"

"My gut told me he was dirty, but I didn't know he was this dirty.

"What are you talking about? What is going on?"

"I can't even think straight", as Lance blurted out while continuing to breathe heavily.

"I don't want to talk about it over the phone," Lance sharply replied.

"Where are you?"

"I'm in Chicago, but I'm heading back to San Jose. I have a crisis."

'Lance, I'm in Phoenix. I'm flying to San Jose from here. I will take a couple days off and meet you there," Candice emotionally replied. "Don't do anything foolish." Candice was worried at this point.

"I won't. I will see you in San Jose."

Lance paced the floor as he waited for the driver to take him to the airport. He booked an emergency flight back to San Jose.

Candice caught a 'red eye' to San Jose. Not knowing where Lance lived, she booked a hotel room at the airport and waited for Lance's flight to land.

[Candice: call me when you land]

[Lance: ok]

Lance called Candice and met her at the hotel. He was still belligerent from earlier that day.

"What is going on? You said you are in a crisis."

"Yes, it's the real estate deal I have been working on over the last six months. I've been working with a snake. He diabolically plans to ruin my company financially if I don't sell him my interest in this soccer stadium deal."

"Oh My God!" Can he do that?"

"Apparently he can and will do it."

"I have 72 hours to decide: the land deal or my company."

"I'm so sorry Lance. I'm so sorry."

"I lose either way. I can't think about this anymore right now. I have to lie down. My head is pounding", as he finished his double Scotch.

Candice held Lance close. She realized that the man from the plane was not just a capricious fling, but also a decent man with relationship potential. He had reached out to her at his highest moment and now he called for her at his lowest point. Lance slept through the night until mid-day.

* * *

[Charlene Phone Rang]

"Hello!"

"Hey Charlie, how are you? What does your schedule look like for the next week through the next five years?"

"What are you talking about Jonathan", she confusingly laughed.

"Come away with me for the next couple of weeks. We will stop in Brazil to see Lucas and from there; no one knows."

"Where is Jonathan? What did you do with him," she sarcastically replied. "This definitely doesn't sound like the Jonathan I know."

"Hey, let's just say I'm in a good mood; perhaps to be in a better mood soon", he casually replied.

"I can clear my calendar," she excitedly responded.

"Great! I will be there tonight. We will meet a business associate tomorrow and then head down to Brazil to visit Lucas in a couple of days."

"Excellent. Do I need to pack light?"

"You should pack very light. Where we are going, we will get what we need when we get there", he chuckled.

Jon departed Chicago for an early morning arrival time in Los Angeles. He called Charlene to let her know when he would be arriving. She was so excited to see him again.

[Sabastian Phone Rang]

"Hey Sabastian, how are you? I will be in town in a few hours. I would like to get together and have lunch."

"That sounds great. I also will be bringing a friend; I would like you to meet."

"Oh really!"

"Yes, we are heading down to Brazil to celebrate."

"Oh Yes! I'm definitely looking forward to partying in Brazil", as he laughed until his laughter turned into a nasty chronic cough.

Charlene, Jonathan, and Sabastian all met at the private club in Beverly Hills. After introductions and pleasantries, all three engaged in conversation. The three had a late lunch and enjoyed their celebration.

Jonathan proposed a toast: "To all those that seize an opportunity, the spoils of victory are great." The three of them continued their conversations and celebration.

"Sabastian, I had a great time. We are going to head out. I will see you in Rio in a couple of days."

"I will see you in Rio in a couple of days," Sabastian echoed.

Jonathan and Charlene enjoyed an intense evening of passionate lovemaking. They enjoyed each other's company as the evening turned into night.

The next morning Jonathan and Charlene relaxed and went shopping. The couple enjoyed a casual day of food and leisure activities.

The following morning, Jonathan and Charlene departed LA with a destination of Rio, Brazil. Jonathan ordered two mimosas to celebrate the trip.

[Here's a toast: To finally getting away!]

"Charlie, you know that information about that company with the software going online soon?"

"Yes, what about it," she curiously replied.

"Well, we are going to make a lot of money when that project hits the market", as Jon raised his glass for another toast with a smug grin on his face.

The couple enjoyed drinks and strawberries shortly after reaching cruising altitude.

The next day Candice visited Lance at home.

"Lance you have to make a decision. I can't tell you what to do but whatever you decide, I support your decision," Candice solemnly replied.

[Lance Phone Rang]

"Lance this is Lucas. Turn on the news", he apprehensively directed.

[This is breaking news: Billionaire venture capitalist Jonathan Westin's private plane crashed 23 minutes into flight. There were five passengers on board including three crewmembers. No specific details for the cause of the crash were given. Authorities are investigating.]

Lance and Candice watched in awe as news reporters followed the story. They couldn't believe this surreal event.

"Lance, Jonathan was heading down to visit. I hadn't seen him in a few years. Now, he is dead," Lucas grievingly replied. "I have to go. I don't know what to say right now. I'm just stunned."

The tragic news spread throughout the business world. One of the pioneers in the venture capitalism business has passed away. Jonathan made a significant impact on several businesses. His firm was responsible for taking several businesses public throughout his career. Because Jonathan lived in the city for many years, the Chicago business community was especially heartbroken by his sudden and tragic death.

Lance received a phone call from Henry Howard, chairman of the board of his company.

"Lance, I really didn't want to make this call. I'm not sure if you heard but Charlene Brooks was killed in a plane crash with Jonathan Westin. It is a tragedy and a loss."

"I didn't know. Thank you for calling", as he hung up the phone. The death of his board member delayed the upcoming release of the company's new software product line out of respect for her family. The company issued a statement.

A few weeks later, Lance's company finally released the software product line. The social media community received Lance's new product well resulting in significant investors' confidence. This investors' confidence reflected in the company's stock price increase of thirty-four percent within a few weeks. The new product line, coupled with the company's quarterly earnings report drove market capitalization to a whopping thirty-eight percent of the media sharing market.

The New York Stock Exchange invited Lance and his

executive team to pound the gavel for the opening bell of the Wall Street stock market.

[Joe's Phone Rang]

"Hello, Joe. This is Lance."

"I know Lance. I have you in my phone address book", as the two of them laughed.

"I will be in New York in a couple of days to open the stock market."

"Wow that is fantastic man."

"By the way, I will introduce you to my friend Candice. We have been 'going steady' over the last few months. I'm going to see how things go. I finally decided to date instead of being a sex beast."

"I can't wait to meet this woman. Our conversations should be interesting", as he chuckled.

Two days later, Lance and Candice arrived in New York. This time, Candice wasn't working. She was excited to be back in NYC.

"Lance, I have a relative I would love to see while I'm in town. You think you could stand to miss me for a few hours", as she put her hands on her hips with a cheesy smile on her face.

"I guess I will manage", as he grinned.

"I will meet you back at the hotel", as she waved and blew a kiss.

Candice took a ferry out to the Statue of Liberty. There she met Joe McGee and Thomas Kent.

"Your money will be in your accounts like we agreed", Thomas callously spoke. "That money was well spent to rid the world of such a prick. I never liked Jonathan. Who says revenge isn't sweet", as he puffed on his Cuban cigar.

"Now let's go and celebrate with our friend: Lance Howard," as the three of them parted ways.

Candice and Joe took the same ferry back. Thomas decided to stay and enjoy the open air a little longer.

"Candice, is Candice your real name", Joe curiously inquired.

"Yes, Candice is my real first name; Campbell, however, is not my real last name", as the two of them laughed.

"I have a couple more questions if you will humor me," Joe requested.

"Ok, what are the questions?"

"I know you are a flight attendant. However, how did you know what to do to make it seem like Jonathan's plane crash was an accident?"

I used my flight attendant credentials to gain access to the aircraft the night before Jonathan's plane was scheduled to depart. I hacked into the private flight manifest system for aircraft that fly into and out of LAX. These flight manifests are stored in a separate database from the normal commercial flights. Like most businesses, their IT firewalls are weak with some businesses still store default administrator's passwords. This system still had default passwords stored. I gained access to Jonathan's flight data.

The mechanical portion of the operation was simple. I accessed the avionic panel that controlled the rear ailerons and attached a liquid detonator to all three of the independent fuel and electric lines. Once the aircraft reached a certain altitude, the drop in temperature triggered a chemical reaction in the detonator. Once the reaction began, the chemicals dissolved through the lines causing a mechanical failure of the ailerons resulting in loss of control of the aircraft.

"Damn, you are the smartest flight attendant I have ever met", as they both chuckled. "Hell, I struggled with algebra. I can't even imagine some of the courses you took in school", as he shook his head and gave Candice a high five.

"Ok, I have a couple more questions."

"What are your questions?" as Candice smirked and rolled her eyes.

"How did you know that Jonathan would be in LA at that time for you to do all the things you did?"

"I wrote a program to gain access to Jonathan's cell phone using Lance's cell phone as an electronic pathway when I saw Lance in Chicago," she keenly replied. I knew he was meeting Jonathan the next day and used that meeting as an opportunity for a clone program to gain access. I got special skills", she remarked as she rested her hands on her hips.

"I am truly impressed with your 'special skills'," as Joe eyebrows raised. Now, it's time for us to celebrate. I guess we both have been looking out for Lance. Although he has been successful in the software business, he was way out of his "league" with the real estate venture", as they both shock their heads and chuckled.

CHAPTER 13

CANDICE Mitchell, also known ask Candice Campbell, did possess brilliant and exceptional analytical skills. Candice graduated from Richard University with a double major in mechanical engineering and computer science. She joined the Army after graduation. The Army offered her a huge sign-on bonus and a generous loan repayment plan for her student loans. Candice qualified for the Army's Special Cyber Initiative Program. As a graduate of the Army's Cyber and Intelligence Operations School, Candice displayed multi-dimensional skills in computer science programming, mechanical engineering, and "street smarts". Candice received an honorably discharged from the Army after serving her four-year commitment. Although her father was a Navy retired flight mechanic, he was very proud of his daughter even if she didn't follow in his footsteps in joining the Navy. Throughout the years, Candice learned a lot from her father about aircrafts. She used those skills, coupled with the skills she learned in the Army, to do freelance work to support her traveling and surfing lifestyle. Candice worked as a flight attendant because the job afforded her the ability to travel to exotic locations. The job also served as the perfect "cover" when she was doing surveillance work.

After completing this last contract job for Thomas, she had worked her last stint as a flight attendant. Now, she would be a passenger and enjoy the ride.

* * *

Thomas relished in his revengeful victory. He had finally gotten 'even' with the man that tried to destroy his first sports team business venture. Thomas knew he couldn't get close enough to Jonathan to render the 'payback' he deserved. When Thomas discovered that Joe McGee knew Lance and that Lance met Jonathan, Thomas saw this meeting as the perfect window of opportunity to get close enough to Jonathan to render his retaliatory wrath. Thomas only needed someone close enough to Jonathan that Jonathan would never considered that person to be a threat. Lance was that "sacrificial guinea pig". Lance, often oblivious, "played" right into the "hands" of the two adversaries in a symbolic but diabolical game of chess.

Ironically, Lance benefited from the death of the sinister villain. Jonathan's attempt to destroy Lance by purchasing the majority of his company's outstanding stocks sent the stock price soaring. Jonathan's sudden purchasing trend led the stock market to follow suit and ride the wave of prosperity. With Jonathan dead, and the stock shares tied up through offshore subsidiaries, it would take years before the heirs to Jonathan's estate gain control of his assets. Additionally, Lance's company latest software product line propelled the stock to unheard of levels. Investors that purchased the stock before the software release, benefited significantly from the market-timed purchases of Lance's stock at bargain prices.

Believing Jonathan's death was an accident, Jonathan's

conspiring partners for the real estate venture were still onboard with their financial commitments. Thomas talked Lance into allowing him an opportunity to invest in the real estate venture. Lance gladly accepted. Thomas saw the venture as good business and an ideal situation to keep a watchful "eye" on Lucas, Vito, and Sabastian.

ABOUT THE AUTHOR

Tony Webber (pen name: Frank Lee Speaking) is a retired US Army Reservist from Columbus, MS. Throughout his professional career, he has worked as a: real estate developer, project manager, Cyber & Intel operations specialist, and an Information Technology (IT) security consultant. He is an alumnus of Virginia Commonwealth University, University of North Florida, and Mississippi State University respectively. While in Baghdad, Iraq, he started writing poetry and short stories to pass the time. He has written over 100 poems. Tony also performs at Open Mic venues in the

Washington DC area. As a lifetime learner and avid traveler, Tony presents a narrative but intriguing writing style. Where the classroom ends and life begins, he writes stories and poems that are amusing, animated, and reflective of his life experiences. "I write for three reasons: For my books to be a testament that anyone can do anything, go anywhere at any time when that person decides in their mind that is what he/she wants; to blaze a trail for others to follow; and to inspire many or just a few that they're only one thought or one day away from changing their lives."

Tony's first book: Tease: The Lace Collection, can be found on his website at www.franklspeak.com